"You mean…" Megan swallowed. "The Earl of Shrafton is now…"

"Nicholas." Felicity finished Megan's sentence.

"I'm not ready. We've got to go now!" Megan stood and took Felicity by the arm.

Megan's friend stood her ground. "Now wait a minute. This is part of the reason you came back to England—to tell him the truth."

"Not now. Not here, not tonight." Megan thought of her son, tucked away in her townhouse at the moment, unaware that his parents could quite possibly come face-to-face for the first time since before he was born. "I can't deal with this right now. I'm leaving."

Pushing Felicity in front of her, Megan started down the hallway. She glanced backward as they exited, turning forward just in time to note that Felicity had stopped short before she slammed into Felicity's back.

Felicity reeled sideways, leaving Megan smack in front of the man she had tried for so long to forget.

Dear Reader,

I hope the long hot summer puts you in the mood for romance—Silhouette Romance, that is! Because we've got a month chock-full of exciting stories. And be sure to check out just how Silhouette can make you a star!

Elizabeth Harbison returns with her CINDERELLA BRIDES miniseries. In *His Secret Heir,* an English earl discovers the American student he'd once known had left with more than his heart.... And Teresa Southwick's *Crazy for Lovin' You* begins a new series set in DESTINY, TEXAS. Filled with emotion, romance and a touch of intrigue, these stories are sure to captivate you!

Cara Colter's THE WEDDING LEGACY begins with *Husband by Inheritance.* An heiress gains a new home—complete with the perfect husband. Only, he doesn't know it yet! And Patricia Thayer's THE TEXAS BROTHERHOOD comes to a triumphant conclusion when *Travis Comes Home.*

Lively, high-spirited Julianna Morris shows a woman's determination to become a mother with *Tick Tock Goes the Baby Clock* and Roxann Delaney gives us *A Saddle Made for Two.*

We've also got a special treat in store for you! Next month, look for Marie Ferrarella's *The Inheritance,* a spin-off from the MAITLAND MATERNITY series. This title is specially packaged with the introduction to the new Harlequin continuity series, TRUEBLOOD, TEXAS. But *The Inheritance* then leads back into Silhouette Romance, so be sure to catch the opening act.

Happy Reading!

Mary-Theresa Hussey
Senior Editor

Please address questions and book requests to:
Silhouette Reader Service
U.S.: 3010 Walden Ave., P.O. Box 1325, Buffalo, NY 14269
Canadian: P.O. Box 609, Fort Erie, Ont. L2A 5X3

His Secret Heir

ELIZABETH HARBISON

SILHOUETTE *Romance*

Published by Silhouette Books

America's Publisher of Contemporary Romance

For Linda Allen, who helped pull me through a tough
pregnancy and never made me see my weight at checkups.

Also, thanks to Elaine Fox and Marsha Nuccio, who helped
pull me through this book with an infant on my lap.

SILHOUETTE BOOKS

ISBN 0-373-19528-1

HIS SECRET HEIR

Copyright © 2001 by Elizabeth Harbison

This edition published by arrangement with Harlequin Books S.A.

® and TM are trademarks of Harlequin Books S.A., used under license.
Trademarks indicated with ® are registered in the United States Patent
and Trademark Office, the Canadian Trade Marks Office and in other
countries.

Visit Silhouette at www.eHarlequin.com

Printed in U.S.A.

Books by Elizabeth Harbison

Silhouette Romance

A Groom for Maggie #1239
Wife Without a Past #1258
Two Brothers and a Bride #1286
True Love Ranch #1323
*Emma and the Earl #1410
*Plain Jane Marries the Boss #1416
*Annie and the Prince #1423
*His Secret Heir #1528

*Cinderella Brides

ELIZABETH HARBISON

has been an avid reader for as long as she can remember. After devouring the Nancy Drew and Trixie Belden series in grade school, she moved on to the suspense of Mary Stewart, Dorothy Eden and Daphne du Maurier, just to name a few. From there it was a natural progression to writing, although early efforts have been securely hidden away in the back of a closet.

After authoring three cookbooks, Elizabeth turned her hand to writing romances and hasn't looked back. Her second book for Silhouette Romance, *Wife Without a Past,* was a 1998 finalist for the Romance Writers of America's prestigious RITA Award in the Best Traditional Romance category.

Elizabeth lives in Maryland with her husband, John, daughter, Mary Paige, and son, Jack, as well as two dogs, Bailey and Zuzu. She loves to hear from readers and you can write to her c/o Box 1636, Germantown, MD 20875.

Dear Reader,

I am delighted to be able to add *His Secret Heir* to my CINDERELLA BRIDES series. As a huge fan of fairy tales, I love having the opportunity to make one up now and then, and to linger in that other world while I write.

This is a very personal book for me. Like the heroine, Megan, I was an exchange student in London about a decade ago. Also like Megan, I had a pen pal I had been corresponding with before I went to England and who became my best friend once I got there, and who has stood by me through thick and thin ever since. I also share Megan's love of that beautiful old city, with its ancient churches, quiet river, bright lights, red buses, rattling tube trains and, of course, Cadbury Chocolate.

Unlike Megan, however, I didn't meet an aristocrat who would become the love of my life, but I had a great time creating Nicholas for her!

It was fun taking a trip back in time, to the city I remember so fondly. I hope you enjoy the ride!

Sincerely,

Elizabeth Harbison

Prologue

"Hello, Megan. I understand you delivered a beautiful baby boy last night."

The woman standing before nineteen-year-old Megan Stewart had cottony gray hair pulled back into a bun. Megan almost took comfort in the woman's kind eyes until she realized who she was and why she'd come.

"You're Mrs. Clancy, right? You're here about the adoption."

"Call me Alma," the woman replied, with a smile that was wholly sympathetic. "And yes, I'm here to discuss your options."

Options. Megan had no options—it was the one thing she was certain of.

"I saw your son," Alma Clancy continued. "He's beautiful."

The words stung Megan's heart. "I haven't seen him."

Alma's face registered momentary surprise. "You haven't seen him?"

Megan shook her head. "I want to, but I'm afraid if I do, I won't be able to…" She couldn't finish.

"Are you having second thoughts about letting go?" Alma sat on the bedside chair and set her brief-case next to her.

Megan felt heat rise in her cheeks. She couldn't allow herself the luxury of second thoughts. She had to think of the baby first. "No," she said, not meeting the older woman's penetrating gaze.

"Hmm. Let's begin slowly." Alma took a clip-board out of her briefcase, and looked at the top sheet. "You've listed the father as 'unknown.'" She looked up. "Is that correct?"

It was far from correct. Megan had thought of al-most nothing but her baby's father—three thousand miles away in England—for the past eight months. Even last night, her dreams had been filled with Nich-olas…and a child. A little boy with dark golden hair and smoky blue eyes like his father's, who reached a pudgy hand—like a tiny starfish—toward Megan.

But she didn't take it. She couldn't, not even in her dream.

She'd awoken with a start to glaring fluorescent hospital lights and sterile white walls. No Nicholas, no baby. No one but her own fractured self.

Is the father unknown? The question hung in the air.

Megan clenched her teeth. Nicholas could never find out about the baby. She'd nearly told him once. Two months into her pregnancy, thinking she had to do "the right thing" by him, she'd written a letter asking him to call, but he hadn't responded. Now she thanked God for that. She could imagine the mighty Chapman family swooping down like vultures, plucking her baby up and carrying him off into the cold darkness that Nicholas had described as his own childhood. She loved this child too much to doom him to that fate.

Megan's fingers curled around the sheets, twisting them into coils. "I...I'm not sure who the father is."

Alma waited a moment, then glanced back at her papers. "It says here that you were on an exchange program in London last fall. Did you meet someone there?"

Yes! Megan wanted to scream. *He comes from an old aristocratic family in England. Nicholas is the Viscount Hennington and his father is the Earl of Shrafton. They have more power than you could imagine and I'm frightened to death that if they find out about the baby they'll take him away and treat him like the bastard child no one talks about. They'd take him because they'd think he was theirs, not because they loved him.*

Megan bit down on her lip and hot tears spilled onto her cheeks. She felt Alma's hand reach down and smooth her hair back and soon she dissolved into choking sobs.

"Shhh," Alma hushed. "It will be all right. We

can work it out. I'm here to help you. No matter what that means.''

Megan glanced around uneasily, then her eyes fell to her hands in her lap. "What if I kept him? Could I possibly protect my son if his father's family came after him?''

"Right or wrong," Alma said pointedly, "it is rare for a family to come in as you describe and take custody away from a good and loving mother. There may be visitation rights, but no, I don't think they could take him away as you fear.'' She looked at Megan kindly and shook her head. "But if you don't mind a little personal advice, important decisions should never be made based on fear. You should always listen to your heart.''

They sat in silence for a long while. Megan looked thoughtfully out the window while Alma studied Megan with a professional calm.

"I want to hold my baby,'' Megan said at last.

Alma looked deeply into Megan's eyes. "Shall I put the adoption papers on hold for the moment?''

"Yes,'' Megan said, feeling she could breathe for the first time in nearly a year.

Alma started to call the nurse.

"Wait,'' Megan said, putting a hand on Alma's forearm. "I'm afraid.''

From somewhere far down the hall came a baby's cry. Megan straightened up in bed. Her breasts were painfully heavy and some milk had leaked onto her nightgown. She tensed and looked up at Alma Clancy. "Everyone told me that it wouldn't be fair to the baby for me to keep him. And in so many ways, I know they're right.''

Megan's parents had been sympathetic, but they'd been adamant that she should give the baby up for adoption. They wanted Megan to finish college and have a good career...the kind of career neither they nor their ancestors had been able to cultivate without a formal education. Sometimes Megan thought that was even more important to them than it was to her.

But at the same time, she believed that they would support any decision that she made about the baby.

Alma raised an eyebrow, waiting. ''And what about you? What do you feel?''

She repeated the list she'd given herself so many times. ''I'm afraid it would be a struggle for him to grow up with a single working mother, that I've caused him enough trouble already, that I've shown such bad judgment so far I have no right to keep him, no matter how much I love him. And I do, I really do.'' Megan tried to smile. ''But I wonder if I should even try to listen to my heart. After all, it's made some pretty big mistakes so far.''

Alma persisted. ''Listen now. What do you really want to do?''

''I—'' She took a breath. She knew, inside, what she wanted to do. She knew, inside, what was best. She'd known all along. She'd just never thought it would be as simple as it suddenly seemed. ''I want to keep my baby.''

Chapter One

Ten years later

He could not believe it.

Nicholas Chapman, also known as the Earl of Shrafton, studied the piece of paper on his desk as if it held his execution orders.

He would have loved nothing more than to crumple the whole thing up and toss it in the trash, but he couldn't bring himself to do it. According to the paper, he was about to be confronted with the one woman in the world he had ever truly loved.

Nothing could be worse.

Megan Anne Stewart was coming to London this semester to teach English, the paper said. On the very program Nicholas himself had established. Nicholas couldn't think of another thing that could have happened that would have caught him so off guard. Tornado ripping through London? He would open the windows and hope the house didn't blow away. Tsunami rising from the Thames? He'd hold his breath and try to swim to the top. Aerial attack by Scotland? He'd take shelter in the nearest tube station.

But Megan Stewart coming back into his life? He was doomed.

Perhaps he should have had some sort of emotional bomb shelter in place, but it had honestly never occurred to him that he might see her again. And even if he had entertained the idea on some level, he wouldn't have anticipated the inordinately strong reaction he was experiencing right now.

It wasn't regret about the past. He'd known when he ended their relationship that he was doing the right thing, and he knew now it had not been a mistake. The mistake had been in letting himself feel too much for her, knowing, as he had, that they could never really be together.

The intercom on his desk buzzed, startling him. He slapped his hand on it without looking up. "Yes, Monica," he said with a weary outpouring of breath.

"Your ex-wife is holding on line four."

His jaw tightened. When it rained, it poured. "Not now, Monica." He raked his free hand through his dark blond hair. "Tell her I'm out."

"Yes, sir."

He lifted his hand from the intercom, thereby dismissing Monica and her rustling pile of messages. The last thing he needed at this particular moment was to be reminded, yet again, of his brief and miserable marriage. Of course, it was impossible to think about Megan without thinking about his marriage.

His thoughts jumped back to the problem of Megan's return. Was it too late to terminate her contract? He looked at the calendar on his desk, though he didn't need to. Of course it was too late. The staff introduction party was this evening and classes began Monday. She was already in London.

He stood and walked to the window, then leaned against the sill, flattening his hand against the cold pane. Raindrops trailed down the glass like tears. Megan's tears he'd never forgotten.

Megan. The name rolled across his mind like a lone marble. She'd been gone so long now that—what? That he'd forgotten? Hardly. He gazed unseeing at the skyline and dingy buildings as a memory drifted into his thoughts: a willowy girl sitting on a bench in St. James's park, under the nail-varnish pink of the London sky at dusk. Her deep auburn hair was knotted into a braid behind her, and her face was exquisitely peaceful as she slept, unaware of the movements of the city around her. Unaware of the besotted young man who admired her from a distance. The image was emblazoned upon his mind, and had been for ten long years.

Nicholas's breath hissed through clenched teeth. He should have left her alone that day. He could have done without her. He *should* have done without her.

Being with Megan had just made his subsequent marriage seem that much emptier. Not that the marriage had been a mistake. It had brought about a very important merger, one that had helped make him number 233 on this year's *Forbes* 400—something his father had never been able to achieve. It was a level of success his father had only dreamed about before Nicholas had come along and made it a reality. That *meant* something, damn it.

Which made it all the more absurd that he was standing here, in an elaborate office amidst his empire, wearing uncomfortable clothes, and fighting the stirrings of a long-quiet heart. Not to mention other, more immediate stirrings. Megan—her American girl freshness, her feminine scent, her soft, satiny skin—had the power to arouse him sexually as no other woman had before or since the time of their affair.

His breath fogged the window, shrouding Regent Street below in mist. In the distance he could see the dome of St. Paul's and his stomach tightened. How many times had he been there with Megan? How many times had he returned after she'd gone? When had he finally stopped?

He had to stop now.

He had to answer any questions lingering in the back of his mind, and let the subject go. Just as he would with, say, an acquisition—or a marriage—that didn't work out.

Why was Megan the one memory that was always so hard to put out of his mind?

He returned to the desk and sat down heavily before picking up the paper to study the short biographical paragraph on Megan. She'd graduated from the

University of Maryland in 1995. 1995? She must have taken some time off. When he'd known her she only had two semesters left. He looked back at the paper. She'd gone on to get her master's degree from George Washington University and had been teaching English literature at a college in Maryland ever since.

Now she was back. Even if he made a concerted effort, it would be impossible not to run into her at some point. What would he say to her?

Lovely to see you again. I'm in a bit of a hurry but we must have lunch sometime. Oh, and sorry about what happened ten years ago…

Would she even remember? It had been so long now; maybe the details had faded for her. Who knew what had happened in her life since then?

He studied the paper for…what? Something between the lines? Some reference to their shared past? Anything that would tell him about her. The inventory of her education and work history gave no clue to her personal life. He didn't even know if she was married. Her last name was still Stewart, but she had always made such a point of how, *if* she ever got married, she would keep her own name and her own independence. She'd had a lot of ideas about independence, Nicholas recalled. He used to pull them out of his memory bank when he needed to remind himself how utterly unsuited she was to life as a British countess.

He looked back at the sheet, wondering if she'd changed her mind about any or all of those things. Perhaps she was happily married; perhaps she even had a brood of children. Perhaps when she had left

England she'd forgotten all about him. Well, after she'd written that letter anyway.

Letter for you, sir. The maid—Nelly? Kelly?—had held a tray out to him with an envelope on it. He remembered with absolute clarity the horrible mix of excitement and then dread when he'd realized it was Megan's handwriting.

He'd read the letter once, though it probably would have been less painful to ignore it altogether. She'd said she felt there was unfinished business between them, that she'd like him to call so they could talk about it. Of course he'd known that calling would only make things more difficult than they already were. Maybe their relationship *was* "unfinished business," but it was doomed to remain so and no amount of talking or bleeding over it would have changed that fact. So he'd tossed the letter, and the phone number, and he'd gone on to do what he knew was the right thing.

No regrets.

He'd done the right thing.

He couldn't afford to spend the next year obsessing about it. There was only one thing to be done—he had to see her now that she was here, had to get it over with.

Tonight.

He pushed the intercom buzzer several times until he heard Monica's answer.

"Yes, sir?"

"Cancel my meetings for this evening. If anyone needs to reach me, I'll be at the university library."

* * *

Megan felt an unusual sense of peace as she stood in the library that night. Either she was finally in the right place, doing the right thing at the right time, or she was even more jet-lagged than she realized. She thought it was the former.

The months stretched long and inviting before her. She couldn't wait to teach eager American students about English literature in a setting so alive with it you couldn't swing a cat without hitting something famous. They would go to Lawrence's Nottingham, to Byron's Newstead Abbey, to Jane Austen's Bath, they would go everywhere, experience everything. Just as she had.

Well, *almost* as she had. These students probably wouldn't get involved with a heartbreaking aristocrat like Nicholas, fortunately for them. The thought of him sent a shudder rippling through her. Like someone walking on her grave, her grandmother used to say.

Megan knew no one had stepped on her grave. The thought of Nicholas made her shudder because there was no more ignoring the fact that she had to find him and tell him about his son.

Not tonight, though, she reassured herself. Tonight she'd concentrate on the fun stuff, the teaching job and the traveling around the country. She'd think about the heavy task of locating Nicholas and telling him about William another time.

The hush of murmuring voices was interrupted by the clanking of a spoon against a teacup. "Attention," a thin, wispy man with lank brown hair and wire-rimmed glasses called.

The room gradually fell silent and all eyes turned to the man, who stood surrounded by a small group of people. "I'm so pleased to see you all," he said. "I am Simon MacGonagle, the director of London Study." There was a polite round of applause. "At this time, I'd like to briefly introduce some of our generous benefactors, who have graciously joined us tonight." He identified a few of the people standing by him, and each got a polite round of applause. Megan was ready to succumb to jet lag when Simon's voice cut through her exhaustion like a knife. "Is the Earl of Shrafton here?"

Megan's heart flipped. Every nerve in her tightened. The Earl of Shrafton. Not Earl the name, but Earl the title. Nicholas's father. It wasn't possible! She'd never heard him described as philanthropic— anything but. She followed Simon's gaze around the room, but no one came forward for the greeting.

She must have misheard.

Megan turned to her friend Felicity, who had come along as moral support, and whispered, "Did he say what I think he said?"

"That's what I heard," she whispered back. Felicity, of all people, would understand the feelings this aroused in Megan. She had been there, witnessed it all from the beginning to the end.

"But Miles Chapman wasn't involved in this sort of thing. Especially not, God forbid, with American students." Megan frowned and ran a hand across her brow. "It would be too much of a coincidence. I mean, there is only one earl of each place, right? There couldn't be two Earls of Shrafton, could there?"

Felicity looked pained. "No, as a matter of fact…"

"Good Lord, do you think it's possible that he would recognize me? The earl, I mean."

"I'm certain he would. In a moment." Felicity took Megan by the arm and led her to a quiet corner. "Listen, Meg, there's something you need to know—"

"Oh, he wouldn't remember." Megan kneaded her hands in front of her. "All in all I was just a small— no, tiny—part of Nicholas's life. His father has better things to do than hold a grudge against me."

"That's a certainty," Felicity said. Her grasp tightened on Megan's forearm. "Now Meg, *listen to me.* He's not here, he's dead."

"Dead?" Megan echoed. William's grandfather dead? "He can't be, Simon just said he was coming."

"Simon said the Earl of Shrafton," Felicity said carefully. "Not Nicholas's father." She leaned slightly closer and repeated the information. "Nicholas's father is dead. He died last year."

Megan's face dropped from wild curiosity to something between fear and concern. "But that means," she swallowed, "that the Earl of Shrafton who would be here is…" She laid a hand to her chest and groped behind her with her other for a chair. She sank into it, took a deep breath and held it.

"Nicholas," Felicity stated, finishing Megan's sentence.

The word seemed to echo around the room, bouncing off walls and descending upon Megan like a tiny cartoon fighter plane. She expelled the breath she'd been holding. "I'm not ready. We've got to go," she said in a low voice. The full impact of Nicholas's possible presence settled over her like a heavy cloak. Her eyes darted to the door. "We've got to go now!" she said urgently. She stood up and took Felicity by the arm.

Felicity stood her ground. "Now wait a minute, this is part of the reason you came back to England— to tell him the truth."

"Not now. Not here. Not tonight." Megan thought of her son, tucked away in a North London town house at this very moment, oblivious to the fact that his mother and father were, quite possibly, about to come face-to-face for the first time since before he was born.

Naturally, William had asked about his father over the years. She'd told him as much as she could about Nicholas, and about their relationship, always making it clear that they'd loved each other but had not been able to stay together.

Recently, though, William's questions had been more specific. He wanted to know things Megan wasn't able to answer—whether his father had played sports in school, how old he'd been when his voice had changed, had he ever broken a bone. Things most kids could learn easily. When he'd asked if Nicholas had ever had the chicken pox, Megan had decided it was time to find Nicholas and tell him the truth. She didn't know why that particular question had pushed her over the edge. Maybe because it was the last innocent question she could answer "I don't know" to, or perhaps it was the greater implication about Nicholas's medical history. Whatever it was, it had made her decide the time had come to tell Nicholas and William the truth.

"It's going to take some careful planning," Megan said aloud.

"Isn't that what you've been doing these past several months?"

Megan tried to swallow the lump in her throat, but it wasn't budging. Her hands shook like dry leaves on a tree. "Yes. But I thought I'd have to spend some time finding him. I thought that would help prepare me to actually see him."

"Well, you found him. Why not just tell him, like jumping into a pool all at once?"

"Not *now*." Megan gathered her breath. "Why didn't you tell me about his father before?"

"Because you specifically told me not to. You said if I ever heard *anything* about him to just keep it to myself, that you didn't want to know and you didn't want to wonder if I knew more than I was saying because I was still living in London. You made me *promise* never to mention him."

"That's true, I know," Megan agreed, then asked, "Do you know more than you're saying now?"

"Only that he divorced soon after marrying. There were no children."

So, William was his only child. His heir. Megan's chest grew so tight she could barely breathe. It was too overwhelming to think about at this moment. She was still half dopey from jet lag. "I can't deal with this right now. I'm getting out of here." She started toward the hallway, hoping no one would notice her as she slipped out. Glancing over her shoulder as they exited, Megan turned back just in time to find that her friend had stopped short in front of her before she slammed into Felicity's back.

And then Felicity reeled sideways, leaving Megan smack in front of the face she had tried for so long to forget.

Chapter Two

He was older, of course, but he had mellowed more than aged. After all, he was only in his mid-thirties. The clear blue eyes now had fine lines fanning from the corners. It was impossible to tell whether they were from smiling or a life hard lived, but they gave his expression more depth than Megan recalled. His mouth was still as finely sculpted as she remembered, curling slightly up on one side, as though he were perpetually amused. His nose, she realized now, was the adult version of William's—straight, strong, dignified. There was also that air of quiet intelligence about him that she'd noticed William assume while constructing Lego blocks or doing his math homework.

Her breath caught in her chest. Could he hear her heart pound? Could everyone? It would give her away. She opened her mouth to speak, but his name died on her lips. She stared at him, powerless to turn away. It happened too fast; it was so unexpected. And Nicholas retained all his former power to melt her bones so that she felt herself transformed into a quivering mass of sensation.

Somehow she'd envisioned her first meeting with him as something she'd have control over. She should have known better. It never worked that way with him.

He stared at her too, but his face didn't mirror the surprise that she felt. The surrounding crowd seemed to recede into darkness and silence. She was aware of nothing but him. Her insides churned with elation and a surprising urge to fall into his arms.

Nicholas. That gorgeous face, so often imagined, with those come-hither bedroom eyes, those powerful, protective arms that she'd longed for. Here he was, looking as wise and kind as the man she had fallen in love with. It was difficult not to embrace him. She knew exactly what it would feel like to wrap her arms around him, to feel his arms tighten around her. She knew what he would smell like, taste like, she could remember it all as if it had been hours instead of years.

"Megan," he said. Incredibly, it wasn't until he spoke that the full impact hit her. His voice had grown only slightly deeper, a bit more husky. Yet she would have recognized it even if she were blind. No one else had ever said her name with quite the same inflection.

"Nicholas," she returned. Her voice sounded surprisingly cold. Suddenly, she was aware of the people around them, and of the fact that many of them were waiting for their chance to speak with the mighty Earl. "How nice to see you again," she said stiffly, with as calm a smile as she could manage. "How are you?"

"Quite well, thanks." He raised an eyebrow, as casually as he might have raised a champagne glass. Seeing her obviously didn't rattle him a bit. "You?"

"Great. Really...great."

The air grew thick between them.

"You look lovely," he said, and it sounded like a moment of weakness because he quickly added, "How long has it been?"

She gave a half-shrug. "Years." *Almost eleven of them. I've got a living, breathing calendar at home, counting off the days like an infinite hourglass.*

He nodded thoughtfully. "Have you been back to England since...the last time I saw you?"

She fought mental images of the last time they'd seen each other. "No, I haven't."

He looked down for a moment—remembering that last time?—then back at her. He cleared his throat and his eyes flickered to someone squeezing past before he looked at her with a gaze so unwavering she felt like they were playing Chicken.

"What made you decide to come back now?" he

asked. It sounded like a challenge, but that could have been her imagination.

Now there's a question that's going to take a while to answer, she thought. *But not tonight.* "Several things. Like the opportunity to give to a program like the one I came over on."

"I'm sure you'll be a great asset to the program." He cleared his throat again and it occurred to her that his apparent detachment might actually be nervousness. She dismissed the thought quickly, though. Nicholas was never nervous. "So what have you been doing for the past ten years?" he asked.

That was a question she could have taken days to answer. Images flew through her mind: Coming home from the hospital with William to live with her parents...the makeshift baby shower her mother and cousin Sheila had put together when they'd learned she was keeping William...long nights of rocking William when she got home from her job as a waitress at Finnigan's Steak House...days of running to the elementary education day care on the college campus between the classes she took and, eventually, the classes she taught...so many birthdays and Christmases and last year her father's funeral after a short illness...yes, she could have taken days to tell him about it. But she wouldn't.

"School, work, the usual."

He nodded, apparently waiting for her to continue, but she could think of nothing to say that wouldn't

open the floodgates to a lot of things she didn't want
to face right now.

"Look," she tried to sound casual, "I'd love to
stay and catch up with you, but I'm just on my way
out now. I'm sure we'll be running into each other a
lot, though, and we'll have another chance." She
gave a brief, forced smile, and started to turn away
from him.

"Wait," he said, with such a commanding air that
she actually did stop.

"Yes?"

"We need to talk."

All at once she was certain their meeting was not
the surprise to him that it was to her. It sounded like
he had an agenda. "Did you know I'd be here tonight?"

"Yes." He'd never been one to play coy. "That's
why I came."

She made an effort to keep her voice low and
steady. "I'm surprised to hear that."

"Why?"

She managed to hold back a sarcastic spike of a
laugh. Instead she met his gaze steadily. "Things
ended rather badly the last time we saw each other."

"Yes." The single word gave no indication of what
he remembered or how he felt about it. "Let's talk."

"Not now."

"When?"

Panic rushed through her. A small part of her felt
like a child going up the first hill of a roller coaster:

I've changed my mind! it cried, *I don't want to take this ride after all, I want to go home!* "I don't know."

"Megan." He reached out and touched her forearm. It was the first time he'd touched her in nearly eleven years. Yet it still sent the same foolish shivers through her. "Please."

"Is this about my job here?" she asked, a little too sharply. She knew damn well it wasn't.

"You know damn well it's not."

She'd never had a good poker face, especially with him. "Then we can discuss it later."

A muscle on the left side of his jaw ticked slightly. She remembered that. He was trying to stay cool. "All right," he said, his voice easing up. "Another time then."

She immediately felt remorse. He had no idea what she'd been carrying around or why she was so defensive now. This was not the way she wanted to introduce the subject of William into his life, or, more to the point, it wasn't the way she wanted to introduce Nicholas into William's life.

She took a deep breath. "I don't mean to be short with you, it's just that I've got to get home to my son." The word was out before she realized it. It had been a long time since she'd thought of William as a secret, to be held back.

"Your son," Nicholas repeated. "I'm sorry, I didn't realize…"

Megan felt a nudge of compassion. He wasn't a monster, he was just a grown-up version of a boy she'd once loved and taken too big a chance with. He didn't know anything about their connection except what he'd witnessed himself. He'd find out the rest soon enough.

"How old is he?" Nicholas asked, interrupting her thoughts.

She swallowed. This was not the time to get into soap opera mathematics. "Too young to be up at this hour, but I'm sure he is, so I really have to go give the baby-sitter a break."

"Of course, I understand. Perhaps next time you'll bring him along."

Megan felt like she'd been struck. It must have shown on her face because Nicholas gave her a curious look, then added, "And your husband too, of course."

"I don't have a husband."

"No?" Something flickered in his eyes, but she wasn't sure what it was. Interest? Disapproval? A carefully cultured courtesy to appear interested even when he wasn't?

"No, it's just the two of us here," she said, trying to stop analyzing him. "And now I really do need to get home, so if you'll excuse me...?"

"Of course." Polite to the core, he stepped aside, but kept his eyes fastened on Megan until an over-eager teacher stepped between them, taking Nicholas's attention and giving Megan the moment she needed to get away.

But his words rang ominously in her mind: *We need to talk.*

They did.

This was really going to happen.

Megan couldn't sleep that night. Every time she closed her eyes, she saw Nicholas. She didn't *want* to sleep because she was scared to death of what her dreams would hold.

Three times she went in to check on William. Each time she sat by his bed and stroked his hair, studying his sleeping face in the half-light coming from the hall. He was beautiful but until tonight she hadn't allowed herself to admit how very like his father he was. Now, as she paused to really look at him, Megan's heart ached at the resemblance.

It was funny how William was so much more familiar than Nicholas. She had thought, until now, that Nicholas was accurately etched in her memory, holding that spot alone. Yet when she'd actually seen him, she'd thought how like William he was—not the other way around.

When she was pregnant she'd worried that the baby might look like Nicholas, that it would cause her unendurable pain to have a daily reminder. She'd been so naive.

From the moment she'd seen William, he wasn't a miniature Nicholas to Megan; he wasn't some poignant reminder of her past. He was life, and joy, and everything good in the world. He represented the future.

Unfortunately, as he'd grown, he'd begun asking questions about his father. How had she failed to anticipate that? Her answers were always vague, that his father lived far away but that he was a very good man. He and Mommy just couldn't work things out and stay together. It was the kind of thing she'd heard a thousand times on TV or in books, and she hated giving the cliché answers, but William was too young to understand the true details.

But as time wore on, the absence of a father grew more poignant. Megan could clearly see the pain in William's eyes after a baseball game, or parents' day at school. Maybe telling Nicholas and William the truth wouldn't bring him a father, but it would at least answer a lot of his questions and hopefully give him some peace of mind on the subject. She had to do it. No matter how hard it would be for her to thread together all the pieces that linked them together.

Giving up on sleep for the time being, Megan stepped down the cool stairway and into the kitchen. The gas fire was on low so she turned the heat up, put a kettle on, and dialed Felicity's number on the phone. Never mind that it was 3:00 a.m., Felicity would understand.

"I can't do this," she said, losing her backbone as soon as Felicity answered.

"Can't do what?" came the sleepy response.

"Any of this. Face Nicholas. Tell him."

"But you will."

"I know." She sighed and leaned against the kitchen counter, cradling the phone in the crook of her neck. "But I don't know where I'm going to get the strength. I thought it would be easier. Now I'm barely into this and I'm completely overwhelmed."

"Why don't you tell me your plan again," Felicity suggested. "Maybe it will help."

"Okay." The kettle started to whistle and Megan went to the stove and took it off the burner. "First I have to get established here. It's absolutely imperative that William is comfortable in England before I do anything else." She put a pinch of tea into an infuser and poured the water over it into a cup. The liquid bubbled in the cup and turned a deep golden brown.

"Agreed. Next?"

"Next I have to get reacquainted with Nicholas." She poured some cream into the tea and stirred the swirl away. "That's going to be tough."

"Maybe it will be easier now that he's not married, though."

Megan gave a wry laugh. "Or harder. At least a wife would keep things a little more impersonal." She hesitated, and stirred the tea some more. The spoon clinking against the cup sounded loud in the otherwise hushed kitchen. "See, this is really bad. Step two of my plan and I'm already stuck."

"No, you're not. You'll get to know Nicholas again. Go out for a meal or two, talk, 'tell me about work,' 'I went to Greece on holiday last year,' that sort of thing, and you'll be more comfortable before you know it. He already said he wanted to talk to you, so it's not as if you have to persuade him.''

"Right.''

"And you don't have to actually locate him like you thought you'd have to.''

"That's true. I've been spared the 'hi, remember me?' routine. Okay.'' She blew some steam off the top of the tea and took a sip. "So assuming I get through a couple of casual chats with him, *then* I have to tell him that Will's his son. Now *there's* an easy conversation.''

"Can't argue with you there, sweetie.'' There was great sympathy in Felicity's voice. "But look at it this way—it will only take a moment to tell him and after you do, it'll be done.''

"And there will be just the fallout to deal with. Maybe *years* of it.''

"You can do it. You've got that book for him, right? The photo album?''

"Yes.'' Megan had put together an album of William, from birth to present, with notes here and there on important firsts. She'd been working on it for years, with Nicholas in the back of her mind. When she'd decided to come to England and tell Nicholas the truth, she'd brought the book along, intending to give it to him if he was receptive to the idea of meeting William.

If he wasn't, she supposed the book would just be

a heartbreaking reminder of how fatherless William truly was.

"Good. That will prove to him that you didn't disregard his feelings completely," Felicity was saying.

"I didn't disregard anyone's feelings."

"I know. This won't be as bad as you fear. And I'll be here for you, whenever you need me."

"Thanks."

"Doesn't help a bit, does it?"

Megan laughed. "No. But I really appreciate you listening to me."

"Any time. You know I'd do anything for you and that sweet boy of yours."

"I'd do anything for him too," Megan said, tipping her head back against the cold wall. "I just hope what I'm doing is the right thing."

The next morning was Saturday and, after finally falling asleep close to dawn, Megan slept until nearly ten. When she got downstairs, William was watching television. He looked up at her and smiled as she came into the room.

"What are you watching there, Will?" she asked, seeing a man dressed as a bee dancing on the screen.

"Some kids' show," William answered. "It's sort of babyish but they have cartoons too. They're really funny—look!" He pointed excitedly at the screen.

Megan followed his gaze and watched the futuristic spy cartoon with him for a few minutes.

William laughed uproariously. "Their accents are so weird!" he exclaimed among waves of giggles.

Megan smiled. There, but for a left turn ten years ago, went William. "Think you can get used to it?" She tried to keep her tone light, but something told her a lot rode on his answer.

He shrugged. "I'm glad we're going home in a few months. I couldn't *really* live here."

It wasn't the answer she'd been hoping for. "Give it a chance," she began.

Their conversation was interrupted by the shrill double ring of the telephone.

"Can you get me a drink?" William called after her as she ran to answer it.

"We don't have servants!" She had only a moment to marvel at the irony before picking up the receiver. "Hello?"

"Hello again, Megan," the rich, achingly familiar male voice said on the other end of the line.

Hopefully he didn't notice her sharp intake of breath. "Nick." *Nicholas,* she corrected herself. *Keep it formal. Stay detached.*

"It was nice to see you last night," he said, and she could tell he was struggling to come up with his words. "It's...been a long time."

She couldn't help but smile, though she was trembling inside. "I think we covered that."

There was an awkward pause during which she realized all at once the obvious fact that they really didn't know each other anymore. "Yes, I suppose we did."

Nervously, she coiled the phone cord around her fingers. He didn't know awkward. "So...what can I do for you?"

"I'm calling to see if you'll have dinner with me tonight."

She swallowed. "Tonight?"

"Unless it's a bad time for you."

I'm afraid it could be. "Well, I'm not sure—"

"Say, eight o'clock? The Fair Maiden?"

He remembered her favorite restaurant. That tiny fact made her shiver. "Wow, is The Fair Maiden still there?" What else did he remember? Why did the fact that he remembered anything at all make her tremble this way? Good Lord, she remembered where *he* liked to eat too. It didn't *mean* anything.

"It's been there for a hundred and fifty years." He gave a laugh. "And I don't think they've changed the menu in that time. Or the peanuts. Certainly not since you were last there."

She dared not try to remember when she was last there. It would have been with him, of course. Under very different circumstances.

"So what about it?" he asked, a familiar smooth persuasion lilting his voice.

"I'm not sure. With my son, it's difficult for me to get away." Which was true, for the moment, but wouldn't be when Mrs. Moran, the housekeeper and

sitter Felicity had found, came back to London tomorrow from her weekend in Ireland.

"You could bring him along."

Megan sighed inwardly and leaned against the cool
wall. It felt good because her own temperature was
rising precipitously. He was the first man in nine
years to ask her on a date and encourage her to bring
William along. It had never occurred to her that he
might be comfortable with kids, or willing to give
even a meal out with one a try. It was quite brave.

And quite considerate.

She didn't know this man, she realized. For years
she'd carried anger for the young man he'd been but
she didn't know him now. "Look, tonight will be
fine. I'll get Felicity to baby-sit."

"Excellent. I'll pick you up at—"

"No, I'll meet you there."

"You always have to complicate things, don't
you?"

Oh, you have no idea, she thought.

And with that, her plan was in motion, ready or
not.

Chapter Three

The evening was cold, windy and damp. An omen, Megan decided ten or fifteen times on her way to meet Nicholas. This wasn't the best time to see him. She should have waited, steadied herself first. Why on earth had she said yes?

Not because she *wanted* to see him socially, that was certain. It wasn't as if he still had that power to captivate her. Once she had been so lured by his charisma that she would have done anything to be with him, but those days were long over. She'd been just a child then. Clearly she'd glorified those attributes in her mind when in reality, she'd been all wrapped up in physical attraction.

Well, she wouldn't have that problem anymore.

Sure, he was still attractive. Almost ridiculously so. She'd have to be a fool to have not noticed that. The important thing was that she didn't have a weakness for it anymore. The only reason her reaction to him tonight had been so visceral was that she hadn't been expecting to see him.

Naturally she'd be nervous the first time she saw him. Or the first few times.

Ideally she'd meet with him a few times and she'd see him as he truly was. Which was in all likelihood just an ordinary man.

Then she'd tell him about William, and she'd tell William about him, and they'd meet, form some kind of relationship, and write letters and visit once or twice a year until William was grown-up and old enough to decide what he wanted to do with the relationship.

It all sounded so easy when she outlined it that way. Too bad she couldn't put all the emotions involved into neat little columns too.

As she walked up High Street in Hampstead toward The Fair Maiden, a chill drizzle blew against Megan, casting further doubt on whether she should be here. She was considering going home for the twentieth time when she heard Nicholas call her.

She turned to see him coming toward her, seemingly oblivious to the weather. He wore faded jeans, a white cotton shirt and a light leather jacket that fit like it was made for him.

Which, of course, it was.

"Hello," she said, suddenly very unsure of herself.

He gave a brief smile, the most fleeting glimpse of those even white teeth that used to make her want to kiss him. "From the reception you gave me on the phone, I thought until the last moment that you might change your mind."

"Well." She let the word drop. There was nothing to say. It had been a distinct possibility and there was no sense in protesting. It was disconcerting that he could still read her tone. Why couldn't she shake the feeling that he knew her inside and out?

"Well." He laughed, the very laugh that had made her heart pound foolishly more than ten years ago. "Let's go in before you do change your mind."

An objection formed on her lips but she let it go. She wasn't turning back now.

They passed a Laura Ashley shop and turned onto what could have been a street straight out of *Oliver Twist*, complete with wrought-iron fencing, street-lamps, and faded signs with Old English lettering.

"Here we are." Nicholas took her arm and led her to the first door on the right. The sign that creaked back and forth on rusty hinges over the door read The Fair Maiden and depicted a peeling painting of a woman in a Victorian snood, holding a candlestick. The red flame of the candle cast a harsh glow on her face and made her look almost sinister.

Megan sighed at the sight of it. It was exactly as she remembered. "That sign always made me feel like I should have brought a wooden stake or a silver bullet with me, just in case."

"I did," he said with a straight face. "Can't be too careful."

"That's true," she murmured before she could think.

A gust of wind heaved its weight against the sign and it creaked. Megan shivered.

"Is it the environment or the company that's making you uncomfortable?" Nicholas asked, opening the door.

"I'm not uncomfortable." The wind rose again and blew her lie to the west. "It's just…it's a little colder out here than I expected."

"Ah."

"But then I should have known better than to try and figure out what to expect in England. Weather-wise, that is."

"Or otherwise." His gaze was inscrutable. He nodded to the open door. "After you."

Inside, Nicholas noted, it was not crowded. A few Edwardian-looking men stood at the bar, a couple with handlebar mustaches, pints of bitter and cigars. It looked like a *Monty Python* set. Small cherrywood tables stood stoically about the room, adorned with ashtrays and cardboard coasters bearing the imprint of a local brewer. The high walls were decorated with velvet flocked wallpaper, faded to a dusty rose and punctuated by brass sconce-style lamps with low-watt bulbs.

In the corner, the table where they'd once sat together was empty. There was a moment's silence as they both obviously pondered it. Then Nicholas gestured to a table by the window instead. "How about there?"

"Perfect."

They sat down and Megan looked out the window, giving Nicholas an opportunity to study her unobserved. She'd changed, a fact which shouldn't surprise him, yet did on some level. In his mind, she'd been nineteen for ten years.

It had probably been gradual, he decided. A slow softening of the eyes, the slight plumping of the cheeks, the subtle redefinition of the lips. He'd wondered, once or twice over the years, what she looked like as she grew older. But instead of satisfying his curiosity, finding out made him melancholy.

He thought of the Megan of eleven years ago. He remembered her surprisingly well, despite his best efforts over the years to put her out of his mind. He could recall the sweet smell of her hair, and what it felt like brushing against his bare skin. Her hair had been soft, just like her skin. His fingers burned to touch her now, but was it true desire or just a need to satisfy some old yearning that had been left unaddressed? If he touched her now, would the need finally leave him or would it ignite into a fire he couldn't control?

The possibility made him very uncomfortable.

"What would you like from the bar?" he asked her, anxious to get a drink himself.

She looked bemused, as though she had been lost in some secret thought. "A half pint of cider."

"Dry, not sweet." It had always struck him as a

metaphor for her strong personality that she preferred
the dry no-nonsense drink to the sweet apple-y variety
most of the girls he knew liked. He called the order
out to the pockmarked man behind the bar.

Megan laughed, then seemed to catch herself.
"That's quite a memory you have."

His memory was a little better than he'd realized.
"My father always said there were three things one
had to do in order to succeed with people—remember
their drink, remember their children's names and remember their secrets."

A look he couldn't decipher crossed Megan's face,
and she looked down at the table. "And are you?
Successful, I mean." She traced her finger along the
cardboard coaster. It looked as if she didn't want to
be here.

"I remembered the drink," he conceded, without
going on to list the other things he remembered. Suddenly there were quite a few.

"You'd have no reason to try and succeed with me,
though," she said, then quickly added, "I mean,
we're not business associates or anything."

"Not precisely." Which begged the question: what
were they? Former lovers sounded so personal. Yet it
was a fact.

Not that it mattered anyway. The evening was already uncomfortable enough without him diving into
the past. He had to keep things current, present. That
was the whole point of coming, after all, to create a
present so that they didn't have to focus on a lot of

baggage from the past on those inevitable occasions that they ran into each other.

With that in mind, he asked, "What is your son's name?"

The ensuing moment of silence was brief but uncomfortable.

"William," she answered after a moment.

"William," he repeated. "That was my grandfather's name. I've always liked it."

"Really?" She looked very surprised. "This was the grandfather you liked, I hope?"

He chuckled softly. "Yes. On my mother's side. He was a good man."

"Good," she murmured, nodding. "That's good."

Obviously it wasn't that interesting to her so he switched the subject back. "Does William look like you? Red hair?"

"No," she lowered her gaze again, "he looks like his father."

"Ah." He nodded, fidgeting nervously with the small paper napkin on the table. "Is he still very involved in William's life?"

Judging from the look on her face, this was a very sore subject. Nicholas was about to retract the question, and apologize for getting so personal, when she answered.

"I'd like for him to be, I think. William would like that. It's tough, though, you know? He's got his own life and I'm not at all sure how he'd feel about taking on a big father role."

Perhaps because of his difficult relationship with

his own father, Nicholas suddenly felt a burst of protectiveness toward this child he'd never met. "This is his son," he said. "How can he feel anything other than responsible for him? Doesn't he *want* to be involved?"

She frowned. "It's not that he doesn't *want* to be involved. He...he lives far away. It's..." she was clearly floundering for the words, "complicated."

"It's also none of my business," Nicholas said. "I'm sorry to have put you on the spot."

"It's no big deal," she said, looking as grateful as Nicholas felt when the drinks arrived. "Fast service," she said, taking her drink from the tray before the waiter could even set it down.

"Should we get menus, or do you prefer to go someplace else for dinner?" Nicholas asked. "This place really isn't as charming as I recalled." In fact, it felt downright cheap. He would have liked to treat her to something better.

"No, this is fine," Megan said. "I'm not really all that hungry anyway, are you?"

"Whatever you prefer."

"I'll just have the cider then."

"Fine." This really wasn't about food, after all, and lobster tail at the Connaught wouldn't have made it any easier to put the past to rest.

"I'm actually glad you called," Megan said, after another strained silence.

This surprised him. "Are you?"

"Yes, I've been thinking we really do need to resolve some things."

He let out a breath he hadn't realized he'd pent up. "It's good to hear that you feel that way. I agree completely."

"You do."

"Absolutely." Although he knew it was wholly inappropriate, he wanted nothing more than to feel her hair, her face, everything he remembered. He laced his fingers before him on the table. "We need to put the past to rest once and for all."

She raised her brow. "I would have thought you'd done that already."

Indeed, he expected the same of himself. He couldn't understand this sudden physical longing. He fiddled with the label on his beer bottle. "I have, of course." He had, he honestly had. "But it's inevitable that we should feel at least somewhat awkward meeting under these circumstances for the first time in so many years."

She nodded slowly. "But you're not suggesting that we…resume—"

"No, no." He had to reassure her on that count. He had to reassure himself, too. "In fact, I was worried that you might think my asking you to dinner was some kind of…I don't know, a ruse to get to know you again."

"Well—"

"It's not."

"I see." She frowned and tapped her fingers lightly on the table before her.

On closer inspection, he could see her hands trembled slightly.

"Still," she continued, "we can't just say, 'okay it's all erased. Let's move forward as strangers now.' We have to talk about our past relationship."

Nothing good could come of that. "Are the details really important?"

"Yes. They are."

She said it with such vehemence that he set his glass down and leveled his full attention on her. "All right then, let's talk about it."

She shifted in her chair, straightened her back, and took a long breath.

He could hear it waver.

"I don't know where to begin," she said, raising a slightly shaking glass to her lips.

Nicholas didn't like this. Why did she want to discuss this if it made her so agitated? What could they gain by rehashing the ugly details of their breakup? "Maybe I can make this easier for you," he began.

"I wish you could."

He leaned back in his chair. "There's no denying that we have a history together, however brief. Naturally it's disconcerting for us to see each other again, as I said before."

"That's true,"

"That's why I called. So we could get this first meeting over and done with. Wipe the slate clean, so to speak." He raked his hand through his hair and shook his head. "Not to become strangers, because it's way too late for that. Just so that if we see each other again while you're here, there won't be this damnable tension between us."

"I have a feeling that's going to get worse before it gets better."

"Why should it?"

She opened her mouth to speak, but then closed it again and sighed before saying, "Never mind. Maybe I'm wrong. I hope I am."

"We're going to see each other, you know. In fact, I've offered my country home in Nottinghamshire to your class for a weekend trip."

Her face paled. "Breybrock Manor? Is that the 'English Manor House' they arranged to take my class to?"

He nodded.

"That trip is in," she thought for a moment, "just a few weeks."

He opened his arms in a wide shrug and was about to point out that was a good reason for them to at least be cordial with each other when her mobile phone rang.

She held up a finger and spoke into the phone for one or two moments before turning it off and standing up. "I'm sorry, that was Felicity. William has a fever, I've got to get home right away."

Nicholas looked concerned. "Is he very ill?"

"I'm sure he's fine." Her voice came in a nervous rush. She was sure he was fine. Felicity hadn't sounded alarmed at all. "But he's sick and he needs his mother. I've got to be there for him."

Nicholas opened his wallet and threw some bills on the table. "Then we have to get you home."

"I'll take the tube," she said, picking up her purse

and giving Nicholas a brief, but she hoped reassuring, smile. "The stop is right by the house."

"I don't care how close the station is to the house, you'll get there faster if I drive you." He took out his keys and put a hand on her arm to guide her out.

"I don't want to be a bother."

"You're not."

She didn't want to *need* him for anything. "Nicholas, honestly, it's not that urgent."

"Really, it's not out of my way," he said. "I have an engagement up there later anyway." As soon as he said it, he realized that it sounded as if he had made a date of some sort, rather than just needing to pick up a contract from a colleague of his. The look on Megan's face confirmed that she'd taken it the same way.

His first instinct was to correct himself, to make it clear that he hadn't made other plans on top of his plans with her. But he stopped himself. His aim, all along, had been to put their relationship on the business track. They'd already tried romance and it had turned out to be the single most painful episode of Nicholas's life. He was no more willing to open the possibility of that pain again than he would be to put his bare hand in a fire. He didn't want to insult her, of course, but if this ultimately helped convince her that he didn't have personal ambitions with her, then that was good. She *needed* to know that. She needed to remember that.

As did he.

Chapter Four

He had an engagement for later anyway.

Megan sank into the butter-soft leather seats of Nicholas's Jaguar and quietly fumed. It was a good thing she hadn't brought up the subject of William's parentage tonight or else they might have been interrupted for Nicholas's other meeting.

Megan replayed the conversation with Felicity in her mind. Felicity had said that William had a fever of just over a hundred but nothing hurt. He was even eating a burger and playing board games. It certainly wasn't a medical emergency. The feeling of urgency came from the fact that he was in a foreign country, probably still a little jet-lagged, and he felt crummy. There was no question that she had to be there.

"Do you want to take him to the doctor?" Nicholas asked, pulling the car smoothly into the traffic on Spaniards Road.

Megan glanced at the clock set in the lacquered wood dashboard. "It's nearly nine," she said, with a little surprise. Where had the time gone? "The doctors' offices are long closed." She looked back at Nicholas's profile, and her heart contracted. Why did the mere look of him send her into an emotional and sensual maelstrom even after all these years?

"If you want him to see a doctor, he'll see a doctor," Nicholas said firmly. "I'll take care of it."

"What, do you have doctors on staff along with lawyers and cooks and parlor maids?" Megan was immediately sorry for her snappish tone but before she could say so he answered.

"Why do you resent that?"

"I don't resent it."

He gave a short laugh.

"What?" She hated how petulant she sounded.

"Obviously you do resent it. You always have. What I want to know is why. This is not a socialist country and neither is yours. I work hard, contrary to what you evidently think, and it happens that I have resources on call, like a doctor I can call to see your son if he's ill. Why should that make you angry?"

It was a damn good question and she had no good answer. "It doesn't make me angry," she said, in a voice that was still too hard. "I appreciate the offer."

"Clearly."

"I do." She sighed and looked out the window at the lights and storefronts gliding by. The answer came to her and she spoke without thinking first. "I just don't want to be dependent on anyone else to take care of my child." That was it, of course. She didn't want to be dependent on *Nicholas,* in particular, to take care of her child. Yet at the same time, the pull to let him take care of things was there. His very presence pulsed with strength and capability. At times it was hard work resisting it.

"Where is *that* coming from?" he asked incredulously. "I merely asked if you wanted me to arrange for a doctor."

"Which I said I appreciate. But if I need a doctor, then I'll call one."

"Very well." He shook his head.

A few moments passed as the car wove in and out of traffic and Megan's thoughts wove in and out of the past. Incredibly, after all these years she still felt a comfortable sense of familiarity sitting in the car with him. It would have been so easy, almost natural, to scoot over, put her hand on his thigh and rest her head on his shoulder. A long time ago, they'd laughed off their small arguments. Tonight, everything went deeper. Megan couldn't recall the old Nicholas without also recalling how he had ended things.

"And I have *not* always resented it." She couldn't stop herself. But she did resent it. His lifestyle was the very thing that had kept them apart; kept him from William.

He tapped his finger on the wheel. "Here we go."

"Here we go, what?" She looked at him sharply, any vestiges of affectionate memory disappearing like smoke in the air. "You asked, so I'll tell you. What I resented was the fact that you didn't tell me who or what you were for the first three months we were seeing each other. I thought you were just an ordinary guy, working as a waiter in a crummy restaurant.''

''I *was* an ordinary guy working as a waiter in a *deplorable* restaurant.''

''You were not. You were a viscount in line for an earlhood, or whatever you call it, just slumming to see how the other half lives.''

''Dom. An earl*dom*.''

''An earldom,'' she corrected impatiently. ''Then when you finally did tell me that, you tagged on the little extra that you were betrothed to some society girl, like some character in a Jane Austen novel.''

''I'm quite sure I didn't use the word 'betrothed.'''

She threw her hands in the air, exasperated. ''Whatever you said, the fact remains that you *were* betrothed. And you married her.''

''That's right, I did. Our families had been planning on it for years. You may consider it archaic but it's a way of merging properties, of making two holdings stronger. My family's honor—my *own* honor— was at stake. I had given my word. People were counting on me.''

She gave a derisive snort. ''Oh, you're an honorable guy all right.''

''Are you saying I'm not?''

She paused and looked out the window. ''I'm not saying anything. Forget it.'' She thought of the letter she'd sent, the fact that he'd never answered, and she tightened her hands into fists in her lap. This definitely wasn't a subject she wanted to delve into right now.

"This was exactly why I thought we should meet tonight." Nicholas's voice was stiff. "So that this—" he gestured toward her with his hand "—could be resolved before we have to be together in the company of other people."

"Well, maybe this can't be resolved," Megan said quietly. "I don't see this conversation ending in any kind of compromise, do you?"

He turned the car onto the sleepy street where Megan's rented town house was. "What's to compromise? I did what I had to do. I can't apologize for that."

"Who asked for an apology?"

He glanced at her. She must have looked more upset than she realized because he softened. "Look, I was wrong to get involved with you when I knew nothing lasting could come of it. For that I do apologize."

"Nothing *lasting?*" She gave a derisive laugh.

"Marriage was out of the question."

"As was common decency, apparently," she said in a tone more acerbic than she intended.

"You would rather I hadn't told you about Jennifer at all? That I just let you go home believing we had a future?"

She looked at him in disbelief. "*That's* what you think the *decent* thing would have been?" she sputtered. "To not admit your lie at all?"

"I didn't lie," he objected. "I never lied to you."

"I think getting involved with me without mentioning the fact that you were engaged to someone else was in itself a lie. Failing to tell the truth all that time was also a lie." She shook her head in disgust. "As far as I'm concerned, there isn't a lot of wiggle room there."

He pulled the car over to the curb and turned to face her. "If you recall, I explained all of that to you at the time."

"Oh, that's right, you lost your head for a few months. You were so infatuated with me, or more likely the idea of running away from your life—"

"I loved you," he said angrily. "Or at least I thought I did."

She shrank back into her seat, feeling like a sullen child. That was Nicholas. He gave, but he took away. At least he was consistent. "You didn't love me. You loved the idea of going against your father."

"If that were true, then I wouldn't have ended it with you, would I?"

Her mouth dropped open. "I see. You loved me enough to leave me."

"I *knew*," he said very slowly and deliberately, "that my family's honor came before my own selfish desires." He straightened his back and gripped his hands on the steering wheel. "I did what I had to do."

Megan bit down on her lower lip, suddenly feeling sorry for the girl she had been, the girl who had hoped for so long that he'd call or show up and make everything right. Then she straightened in her seat. Self-pity was ugly. She wasn't going to indulge in it. "And I did what I had to do," she said.

He looked puzzled. "So there's no problem."

She took a short breath, feeling like a boxer who had just gone sixteen rounds. The quiet in the car was almost deafening. "None at all."

"Which house is it?"

She pointed. "Forty-two. With the red door."

He put the car in gear and drew up several houses before shifting into park and turning back to her. "This didn't exactly go as I'd hoped."

She shook her head. "It wasn't what I'd planned either."

It began to rain. Large drops splashed onto the windshield and bounced off the hood.

"I'd better get in," she said. "Thanks for the cider. I'm…" She wanted to say something—anything—to smooth things over but she couldn't find the words. She'd meant everything she said. She couldn't apologize for any of it.

"I'll walk you to the door," Nicholas said, unfastening his seat belt.

"No, I'd rather you didn't." She pushed the spring and her seat belt came undone. "See you later." She got out of the car before he could answer.

"How's Will?" she asked, as soon Felicity opened the door. "Where is he?"

"He's fine," Felicity answered soothingly. "His fever broke and he fell asleep about ten minutes after

I talked to you. I tried to call you back and tell you not to rush home but there was no answer.''

"Really?" Megan frowned. "That's weird. I must have turned my phone off instead of just disconnecting it. Let me check." She looked for her purse but she didn't have it. "Did I bring my purse in?" she asked, looking at the foyer table where she usually left it.

"I didn't notice," Felicity answered.

"Oh, no." Dread washed over her. She hadn't made that hasty and admittedly curt exit from Nicholas's car and then left her purse inside, had she? Could she have done something so foolish? She opened the front door and looked out at the rain-slicked sidewalk and street to see if she'd dropped it on her way in.

It wasn't there.

"Good Lord," she groaned, closing the door.

"Left it in his car?"

"Yup."

"You know, psychologists would have a lot to say about that." Felicity smiled knowingly.

"I didn't do it on purpose," Megan disputed. Even her deepest subconscious would have known better than to do that. Wouldn't it?

"If you say so." Felicity gathered her things together and gave Megan a smile. "But either way you're going to have to see him again soon."

Megan sighed.

"I guess it didn't go very well."

"That's an understatement."

"Whose fault?"

"Both of ours. Mostly mine, maybe."

"So you left your purse in his car." Felicity nodded. "That makes sense. You don't have to call and apologize, precisely, you can just ask for your purse back."

"It looks like I'll have to."

Felicity put her hand on Megan's shoulder and gave her a quick peck on the cheek. "Maybe things will go better the next time you see him. I'm glad to take care of William any time you want, okay? Get this stuff with Nicholas straightened out."

Megan tried to smile. "I'll do my best."

"You'll have to," Felicity said, opening the front door. "There's a lot riding on it."

Megan stood in the hall for a few minutes after Felicity had gone. It was true, there was a lot riding on Megan's actions. She'd acted like an immature fool this evening, fighting with Nicholas like the teenager she once was instead of talking to him like the adult and parent she was now. The past really wasn't at issue. Whether he'd been right or wrong to marry Jennifer, whether Megan should have tried harder to contact him when she was pregnant, whether he should have answered her letter…all of that was water under the bridge. None of it had any bearing on their present situation.

She looked at the clock, then remembered Nicholas had said he had another appointment tonight so he wouldn't be home yet anyway.

Obviously he hadn't believed that his meeting with Megan would last very long or, by extension, be very interesting, if he'd made other plans for afterward. It was a perfect illustration of how he regarded her, as if she needed that reminder.

She'd just wait until morning and call him at his office. The school would undoubtedly have that number, and calling him at work instead of at home would keep them on the businesslike level he clearly preferred.

With that plan in mind, Megan turned off all but one of the downstairs lights and headed up the stairs to William's room.

He was deeply asleep when she went and sat on the edge of the bed. Outside, a clock struck the half hour but the sound didn't rouse him.

"Mommy's home, sweetie," she whispered, laying a hand to his forehead. It was cool. She stroked his hair and he made a snuffling noise like a baby sleeping. She laughed softly and kissed his cheek.

"Mom?" he asked, opening sleepy eyes.

"I'm here."

"I didn't feel so good." He yawned and stretched, then flopped his arms onto the mattress at his sides. "Felicity said I had a fever but that it wasn't a big deal fever."

"That's right." She traced her finger across his brow. "It's gone now. How do you feel?"

"Okay, I guess. Kind of cold."

She looked at the old radiator under the window.

"The whole house is a little cold. I'll try and turn up the heat."

"The whole *country* is cold," William said, snugging down under his blankets. "I want to go home."

She had been afraid something like this might happen. "For the next few months you are home."

"I mean I want to go *home* home. To Maryland."

"I know what you mean," Megan said steadily. "But I have an obligation to stay here and teach these two semesters and I'm going to. We talked about this before we came."

"That was before I knew what it was like. The house is freezing, it's always raining, the pizza's terrible, and everyone talks funny."

"It's not always raining," she said, correcting the one thing she could. "That's a myth. It just so happens that it's been a rainy couple of weeks since we arrived, but it will brighten up and when it does I guarantee you'll feel better about it."

"What if I don't?"

She wondered the same thing. "You'll have to get used to it."

He rolled onto his side, pulling his blankets with him. "I don't want to get used to it," he said into his pillow.

Megan reached out and scratched his side, a gesture that always soothed him. "Then you're going to be one pretty miserable guy."

He sighed heavily. "I'm already miserable," he said, with fading conviction.

"You're going to love it here, you really are. It just

takes some getting used to. Before you know it, it'll feel like home and you might not even want to leave when it's time." By then he will have met Nicholas, she thought. By then, God willing, he'd have a father.

Maybe that would make it easier for him to stay, or perhaps to make short visits in the future.

William fell back asleep within a few minutes and Megan was in the hall on her way to her room when she heard the doorbell ring.

She looked at the clock as she hurried down the hall. It was eleven.

It was probably Felicity, Megan told herself to ward off visions of police or maniacs banging at her door. There was one more quick ring of the bell and she called out, "I'm coming!"

She made sure the chain was secure and opened the door a crack.

It was Nicholas.

Her heart skipped, undoubtedly from the shock of seeing a man standing there. And not just any man, the part of her that insisted on emotional honesty reminded her. It was only Nicholas who accelerated her heartbeat and made the blood racing in her veins feel like liquid fire.

"I saw the lights on." He held out her purse like it was a dead thing he'd found on the sidewalk. "You left this in my car."

"Oh, thanks." She reached her hand through the crack in the door and took it.

"Megan."

"Yes?"

"I'd like to finish our conversation from earlier."

"I'm not sure we can talk about that civilly."

"We need to try."

He was right of course. More so than he knew. They did need to try again, until they reached a point where they could speak amicably. "Now?"

He shrugged. The rain was soaking him, like some romantic hero from a Brontë novel. "Can I come in?"

She hesitated, thinking immediately of William upstairs. What if he came down while Nicholas was here? The thought made her shudder. A thousand scenarios rushed through her mind, none of them good. But William had been sound asleep when she'd left him. He'd probably stay that way for the night.

"I won't stay long," Nicholas said, after a moment's silence. He turned out his hands in a beseeching gesture, and his fingertips brushed hers. Megan felt as if an electric current had leapt from his touch to change her entire being. It had been the slightest of touches, a mere grazing of his flesh and hers, and yet her body seemed suddenly on fire with memories of all the ways he had touched her in the past...

"It's not that, it's just my son's asleep and..." She stopped. It would be easier to let him come in for a few minutes than to try and refuse. She nodded. "All right." She shut the door and took a deep breath before removing the chain and opening it up again. "Come in."

Chapter Five

"You know, the wrong kind of person could have shoved the door wide open just now," Nicholas said, coming into the foyer. "That flimsy chain wouldn't have stopped them."

Megan gave a wry smile, trying to ignore the way her heart leapt at seeing him again. "I suppose you have a security expert on call too, right? Someone who could pop over and wire the house."

He splayed his arms. "I'm not offering to help, mind you, just making an observation."

"Thanks. I'll slide an armoire in front of the door when you leave."

"Good idea."

She led him into the small sitting room and offered him a seat on the sofa. "I'd like to offer you something to drink but—"

"I don't want anything." He didn't sit, which was just as well since he looked too large and far too regal for the worn rented piece of furniture. "Like I said, I won't stay long."

"Okay." Megan perched on a wingback chair by the door, mindful of any stirrings she might hear at the top of the stairs. "So what did you want to talk about?"

"First, how is your son feeling?"

His concern touched her, but she tried to convince herself he was just being cordial.

"He's fine. Absolutely fine. Felicity tried to call back, in fact, but," she shrugged, "I didn't hear my phone because it was turned off."

He smiled. "I'm sure you're relieved."

"Very." She nodded, waiting.

"I don't like how we left things earlier," he said.

There it was again, that commanding air of his. *He* didn't like how they'd left things, so "things" must be remedied. Was it born or bred? Every once in a while, William managed the same tone.

"What do you want to do about it?" she asked, just as she might have asked William. But, unlike with William, she held her breath waiting for the answer, as if every word Nicholas said could have an enormous impact on her emotions.

"I want to take you to a premiere in the West End tomorrow."

"What?" She felt like she'd missed some vital piece of the conversation. "What are you talking about?"

"Sir Nigel Drake is opening a new production of *Pygmalion* at the Haymarket, and the premiere is tomorrow. There's a small dinner at Pendragons afterward. He was a good friend of my father's so I have to go, and I'd like for you to come with me."

There were probably plenty of people who found it difficult to say no to Nicholas, Megan noted. His eyes had a way of getting straight to a person's gut. If that weren't enough, he had a smile that could persuade Alaskans to buy snow. Besides, the way he carried himself suggested that he knew exactly what should be done and anyone was better off listening to him than to their own feeble inner voices.

There were probably a lot of women who fell prey to all of that in Nicholas, but Megan wasn't one of them. She was *determined* not to be one of them. It was the play she was having trouble saying no to, she told herself. Sir Nigel Drake was a living legend. He was not only famous all over the world for his stage work, but he'd been in quite a few movies—although not one title came to Megan at the moment. Still, opportunities like this didn't come along very often, if at all. And since it was absolutely necessary for her to establish a cordial relationship with Nicholas, this might be the perfect way to do it. If the conversation got too strained, they could always talk about the play.

"That sounds really nice," Megan said, trying to sound as though she'd had this sort of offer from a powerful, gorgeous man she used to be in love with before. "I'd love to go."

He looked slightly surprised. "Excellent. That's that then." He moved to the doorway and seemed to fill it with his presence. "I'll pick you up here at half past six tomorrow."

"Is it for—" Footsteps sounded overhead. Megan froze.

Nicholas smiled and glanced upward. "Late for him to be up, isn't it?"

Megan nodded and swallowed hard.

"I never liked to go to sleep either," he said. "My nanny had a devil of a time getting me to stay in bed at night. But once I did go, it was even harder trying to get me up."

"Sounds familiar," she said vaguely, moving toward the door like a sheepdog herding Nicholas out. She kept half her attention on the stairway. The footsteps had stopped. With any luck, William had realized she'd heard him and had gone back to bed to avoid getting into trouble. "I mean, I think all kids are like that."

"Probably so." He stopped at the door and turned back to Megan. "I'm glad you agreed to come with me. I hope you won't be sorry."

"Why would I?"

"Could be dull," he answered with a shrug. "You never know about these things."

"I seriously doubt it will be dull." Things with Nicholas had never been dull, that was one thing she could say honestly. "I mean, I've always loved George Bernard Shaw."

"You always were a romantic."

"A romantic? I don't think so."

"Of course you were." He laughed. "Do you remember when we went to St. Bartholomew's church because you had to do a paper and you made up an entire history for an eighteenth-century couple who were married there?"

"That wasn't romantic, it was imaginative. They're totally different things."

His mouth turned up into a half smile. "It was romantic."

"Even if it were, which it wasn't, I myself am a very realistic person." *I've had to be.*

He took a step toward her, then stopped, but looked so deeply into her eyes that she felt like she'd been touched. "Can't you be both? Romantic and realistic?"

She shook her head. "They're mutually exclusive."

"You're more cynical than you once were," he observed.

"No, just more realistic." She smiled. "You *can* be cynical and realistic."

"I give. You're the word specialist. All I know is that you're not the same girl you used to be." He cocked his head slightly, studying her. "But you've become a very interesting woman."

Five quick thumps overhead stopped Megan's heart. "I'd better go get him back into bed," she said with an apologetic smile. Though Nicholas was still standing in front of the door, she backed a couple of inches toward the steps, ready to barricade the way, if need be, so that William didn't come running down. "Thanks again for bringing my purse back and for the invitation."

"You're welcome." Nicholas opened the door and stepped out into the evening air. "I'll see you tomorrow then."

She nodded quickly. "Six-thirty. I'll be ready."

She moved forward and closed the door behind him, then watched through the window as he walked to his car. She didn't let out her breath until he had actually gotten in and shut the door. Laying a trembling hand to her chest, she slumped against the doorframe, her heart pounding so hard it scared her.

What would have happened if William had come downstairs? Probably nothing. They would have eyed each other as any strangers would have in their various roles; Nicholas would have made polite conversation, William would have reacted with his typical shyness, perhaps staring at the floor as he often did with strangers, and Nicholas would have left anyway. It wasn't like there would be a dramatic moment of recognition between the two of them.

Would there?

Of course not. All that stuff about genetic memory and psychic feelings was piffle that sold books and got people to watch TV shows. It didn't happen that way in real life.

Feeling better, Megan heaved off the doorframe and turned to go in, only to run smack into a white pajama-clad William.

"Good Lord!" She reeled back. "Willie, you scared the stuffing out of me."

He laughed. "Didn't mean to. I just came down to see who that guy was."

That was reasonable. He hadn't been expecting anyone and neither had she.

"That was the guy I went out with earlier. Nicholas." *Your father, as you'll discover soon enough. The nameless man I've described to you in such detail.* "I left my purse in his car and he brought it back for me."

"Is he your old boyfriend?"

"Yes." Megan took a long breath and thought of how close they'd come to meeting. Soon. But not now. "Yes, he was."

"What's his name?"

"Nicholas Chapman."

William raised his eyebrows in exactly the same way Nicholas did when he suspected there was more to be said. "Do you still like him?"

This was tricky ground. Anything she said now might come back to haunt her later. "He's a nice man."

"But do you *like* him like him?"

She ruffled his hair and tried to smile. "You're the only man in my life, buddy, if that's what you're getting at."

William shook his head and mock sighed. "You're going to have to get a boyfriend eventually. I won't be around forever, you know, I'll have to move out when I go to college."

A pinprick of melancholy stung her. "Let's think about your college career later. Last time I checked, you were still ten." She put her hand behind his thin shoulders and guided him to the foot of the stairs.

"So did you go out with him for a long time?"

"Who?" As if she didn't know.

"*Nicholas.* We were just talking about him."

She hesitated. "Several months. Not all that long." She reconsidered the message that would send when eventually he learned Nicholas was his father. "Well, the whole time I lived here before."

"Why didn't you marry him?"

It was amazing how children managed to hit the right nerves in situations like this. "I had to go home." More truth for groundwork. "And he married someone else."

William stopped and turned to face her. "You went out with a *married* guy tonight?"

"He's not married anymore."

"Oh. Good." He leaned against the bannister. "Are you going to see him again?"

"As a matter of fact, he's taking me to a play tomorrow night."

William made a face. "Boring."

She laughed. "Good thing he didn't ask you then. Now, come on, off to bed."

He resisted. "Wait. Tell me more about him."

"Another time. You need to get to bed now."

"But if you're going to go out with him, I should know something about him."

"I'm not going out with him, Will, I'm just going

to a play with him tomorrow night. He's—" She stopped. "You're just trying to stay up, aren't you?"

The look on his face said *caught!* He burst out laughing. "No, I'm not!"

"Yes, you are." She reached out and tickled him under the arms. "You'd talk to me about the telephone book if it meant you could stay up later."

"Uh-uh," he objected, trying to wriggle away but weakened from laughing.

"Uh-huh." She laughed herself, letting off a world of tension. "You don't care one whit about who I'm going out with or not going out with."

"Yes," he tried to catch his breath, "I do."

"No." She tickled some more. "You don't."

"I do," he shrieked between giggles, "I want to know all about him if," he lost his breath to laughter and tried to squirm free again, "if he's gonna be my new father."

Megan recoiled as if she'd been struck. He was kidding, of course. He'd made jokes like that before when she'd gone out on dates. If he'd been referring to anyone else, she would have taken it in context and thought nothing of it, but this was Nicholas he was talking about.

"What's wrong?" William asked, still woozy with laughter.

She forced a smile. "Nothing's wrong, it's just very, very late. Now get to bed."

"Okay, okay." He was still smiling and gave a half chuckle. "It was worth a shot."

Oh, it felt like a shot all right. "You nearly got

your way," she said, kissing his cheek. "Rascal. I love you."

"Love you too," he said, traipsing sleepily up the stairs like Christopher Robin.

She watched him go and thought of all that Nicholas had missed. Those late nights when she'd led the small boy to his room and read him *Goodnight Moon* over and over until he finally gave up and fell asleep.

My nanny had a devil of a time getting me to stay in bed at night.

How many other similarities were there?

Realizing she wasn't knocking off any time soon, Megan made herself a cup of herbal tea and sat in the dark front room, looking out at the quiet street.

It was strange how much like home this felt. When she'd first come for college, she'd had a hard time adjusting to the differences. It had taken her a month to get used to her daily routine. Yet this time, she'd suffered almost no jet lag and she'd been able to relax in the modest town house on the rented furniture right away.

William hadn't had it so easy. He'd had trouble sleeping at first and he still hated the food so much she was worried about meeting his nutritional needs. He barely touched anything she made because he thought all the English ingredients "tasted funny." She had better luck taking him out for restaurant meals, but she could hardly afford to do that once every few weeks, much less enough to keep him from starving to death.

She couldn't help but think about the fact that

Nicholas would be financially able to take William out for three square meals a day. It made her feel inadequate in comparison, despite the fact that she knew this was not a situation that welcomed such comparisons.

But William was a ten-year-old boy. What would happen if he made the comparisons? It wasn't that she doubted William's love or his ultimate loyalty, but if *he* were faced with a choice of Nicholas's glamorous lifestyle or Megan's modest one, he'd be hard-pressed to forgo the promise of huge houses with swimming pools in favor of tiny houses and the YMCA.

Megan herself could see the temptation.

She set her tea down and stood up. It was time for bed. Time to stop thinking about all of the things that *could* or *might* happen when she told Nicholas about William. She resolved to do it, but she had no control over what happened from there. With any luck they *would* form a close bond. With any luck, William *would* have the opportunity to enjoy the spoils of his own heritage.

She turned off the lights one by one and went up the stairs, hesitating for just a moment in the front hall. She thought that she could still smell Nicholas's aftershave, but it was just her imagination. He was on her mind because of William, there was no other reason.

Soon she would tell him the truth.

Maybe even tomorrow night if the opportunity presented itself.

Chapter Six

"When's he due to arrive?" Felicity asked the next evening, as Megan paced the sitting room watching for Nicholas out the front window.

"Any time now," she said. Actually, he was due in four minutes, but she wasn't counting. She'd just happened to notice the time on the mantel clock.

Felicity sat down on the sofa, looking more relaxed than Megan could even imagine feeling. "You excited?"

Megan shrugged, trying to affect the kind of nonchalance she wanted to have tonight. "Kind of nervous. This is Sir Nigel Drake, after all. I've never met a celebrity before."

"You sure it's Nigel Drake that's making you nervous?" Felicity raised an eyebrow questioningly.

"Of course. What else would it be?"

Felicity ran her fingertips along the arm of the sofa, watching them instead of Megan as she said, "We-ll, we haven't really talked about the possibility of you getting back with Nicholas…"

"There's no possibility of that." Megan's voice was hard. Harder than she felt.

Felicity met her eyes. "Why not? He's free, you're free, you have a child together."

"Because it ended a long time ago," Megan said firmly. "I'm not going backward."

"Would getting together with Nicholas really be going backward?" Felicity asked. "Or would it be moving forward at long last?"

Megan gazed out the window. "He didn't even answer my letter. He didn't have the thimbleful of respect for me that that would have required. How could I be with a man who felt that way about me?"

"I don't think he felt 'that way' about you," Felicity said. "Who knows the real reason he didn't answer? Maybe he didn't even *get* the letter."

Megan shook her head. "He got it."

Felicity sighed. "So what if he did? That was then, this is now. Things are different. Why not start over? It's obvious you still have a thing for him."

"Are you *kidding* me?" Megan gasped. "I feel *nothing* for him anymore." She lowered her voice. "*All* of this is about William."

"If you say so."

"I do."

"The lady doth protest too much, methinks. But all

right." Felicity held her hands up in surrender. "It's just something you might want to think over."

"There's nothing to think about."

"Mom!" William called from upstairs. "That guy's here. In a *huge* car!"

Megan turned to the window just as an old-fashioned limo pulled up. "Oh, good Lord," she said, fighting a small twinge of awe. Things like this just didn't happen in her life. Not even when she was with Nicholas before, when he'd been trying to live an "ordinary" life, before stepping into the grand role someday, of earl.

Felicity came up behind Megan and gave a low whistle. "Pulling out all the stops tonight, isn't he? Hmm, I wonder why?"

Megan shot Felicity a look. "I know what you're implying and you're wrong."

"I didn't say a word."

"You didn't have to." Megan wanted to feel calm, like the glitz and the glamour of the upcoming evening didn't faze her a bit, but the truth was that a childlike voice in her was squealing with delight. *Oooh, look at that gorgeous car!* it said. *I wish everyone in the neighborhood at home could see me now!*

She was a little impatient with herself for feeling that way. This wasn't about her, after all, it was about William, as she'd said time and again. Her interaction with Nicholas was just business and it shouldn't have made a whit of difference whether it was taking place in a fast-food restaurant or a big black limo.

This was all to get to know him again, she reminded herself for the umpteenth time. To warm their relationship up just enough to tell him about William. But when? Tonight? She shuddered at the thought, yet couldn't dismiss it.

She couldn't even guess what his reaction would be if she told him now, and she wanted to be ready for it. Maybe he'd understand and agree to slowly enter William's life. On the other hand, maybe he'd be furious and make custody threats. She no longer feared that he'd be able to take William away from her, but that didn't mean she wanted to face that kind of fight.

But she was jumping the gun. Perhaps when she told Nicholas the truth, it would work out all right. Somehow.

"Do you want me to get the door?" William asked from the hallway.

"No!" Megan felt a chill run through her as she went to him and stood in front of the door, effectively barricading him from it. "I'll get it, sweetie, you just give me a kiss goodbye now."

Fortunately Felicity was right behind William. "I thought we were going to make some hot chocolate," she said, distracting him from the subject of his mother's date. She gave Megan a quick wink. They had already devised a plan to keep William clear when Nicholas arrived.

"And apple crisp?" he asked eagerly, glancing at Megan for approval. "With vanilla ice cream?"

She nodded. "This once." She would have agreed to let him have Pop Rocks and syrup for dinner if that was what it took to keep him out of Nicholas's sight this evening.

Felicity put her hands on William's shoulders to steer him down the hall, and said brightly, "I can't wait. Now let's get going. Bye, Megan, have a good time."

"Bye, Mom." He broke free of Felicity's grasp and ran to give Megan a quick peck on the cheek before disappearing into the kitchen.

"Bye!" she called after him, a little louder than necessary. Nerves, she concluded. They'd steady soon enough. Taking a deep breath, she opened the door, only to have the wind knocked out of her again.

Nicholas had always been attractive. Commanding, even. But standing tall on her doorstep with a light wind rustling the leaves behind him and carrying the light scent of his aftershave to Megan, he was absolutely devastating.

He wore a fitted black tux that made him look like something straight out of a Cary Grant movie. It was vintage 1940s, wide at the shoulder and tapering neatly to a narrow vee at his waist, with a shawl lapel and houndstooth vest. His hair gleamed like burnished gold, his skin tawny, in the light of the streetlamp.

She must have stared just a moment too long because his expression changed from bland confidence to self-consciousness in a matter of seconds. "What's wrong?"

"Nothing. Nothing at all." She instinctively smoothed her simple silk dress, horribly aware that it was not only off the rack, but it had been on sale.

"Is…" She wanted to ask if she was dressed appropriately, but she was embarrassed to. "I'm ready."

"You look great." He held the door open for her as she stepped out.

She wanted to turn back, to go inside and watch television for the night instead. She had no business going out to a fancy premiere in the West End and then to dinner with one of the most famous actors in the world. What had she been trying to prove by accepting Nicholas's offer? That she was sophisticated enough to fit into his world? Well, she wasn't, not by a long shot.

Despite their history, despite the fact that they had once been intimately familiar with one another, despite the fact that they had a child together, Megan was as nervous standing in front of Nicholas now as she would have been standing in front of a judge if she'd gotten caught shoplifting.

"You really do look lovely," he said, coming close enough to put a hand on her arm. He didn't touch her but she was as aware of his proximity as she would have been if he'd kissed her.

"Oh." She pushed her hair back out of her eyes, in a gesture of nervous self-consciousness. "Thanks."

"I always liked you in blue."

Her face grew warm. She hadn't dressed to please him, she told herself. But at least his reaction proved she wouldn't look wildly out of place. "You look nice too," she said. They were black and blue, she thought as they approached the car. How appropriate.

The driver rushed to open the door, but Nicholas stopped him with the smallest gesture, sending the man shuffling back to the driver's seat.

Nicholas opened the door for Megan himself. "Sorry for the ostentatious car. I know how you hate this kind of thing, but it's just so much easier to have a driver on an occasion like this."

"I don't mind it," she said, frowning. It wasn't the first time he'd said something about how much disdain she had for his lifestyle. Had she really been so judgmental? She slipped into the warm interior of the car and sank back against seats more plush than her father's favorite recliner at home. *This is fabulous,* she thought to herself, then thought, *William would have a blast with it.*

Nicholas got in, shut the door, sat opposite her and signaled the driver with a single tap on the privacy window. As the car started moving, he settled back in his seat and studied Megan with frank curiosity. "So tell me, why did you come tonight?"

His question put her immediately on guard. "Didn't you want me to?"

"I wanted you to, yes. But I'm wondering why *you* wanted to. You've made it pretty clear that you don't think much of me."

She shifted. "I don't think I said that."

"You didn't have to." He opened a small compartment in front of the door and a gust of cool air came out along with a bottle of champagne the likes of which she'd only seen in movies.

"You're mistaken," she said. The ride became so

quiet when she stopped speaking that when he popped the cork from the bottle, she jumped.

"Am I?" he asked.

"It's not that I don't think much of you, Nicholas, it's that I don't know you."

"You did once." He took two glasses out and held them in the air, raising his eyebrows in query.

"I don't think so."

He started to put the glasses away.

"I mean I don't think I really knew you," she said quickly. "Champagne would be great." More than great, it would be manna from heaven.

He gave a half smile and poured neatly into the two flutes, untroubled by the bumps in the road. Obviously he'd done this before. "There you are." He handed a glass to her and when she took it, tipped his against it. "To our secrets."

"What secrets?" she asked nervously.

He gave a casual shrug. "We've all got secrets, haven't we?"

"I suppose." She took a sip of the champagne, her hand trembling slightly, then asked, "Are you thinking of something in particular?"

"Only that you just said you never really knew me." He watched her closely, as calm as could be. "Are *you* thinking of something in particular?"

He'd always been able to read her so easily. "No, no. It's just the way you said it…"

He kept his eyes on her. "Yes?"

Her face grew warm again and she was grateful it was too dark in the car for him to be able to see.

"Well, it's an interesting subject, don't you think? What people keep hidden. And why."

"I suppose." A small smile played on his lips. "Often the 'why' is more important than the 'what.'"

"Not all the time," she murmured and took another sip of champagne.

He leaned forward, which put his face just a few inches in front of hers. "You know, I wanted to share this part of my life with you." He was so close, she could feel his breath against her lips. Her pulse raced, and her insides melted like butter.

She understood what he was saying. "And I wanted to know everything about you."

"Funny thing about near misses. Good with airplanes, but not so good with people." He smiled, but it faded quickly as he studied her face, her eyes, her mouth. "People can waste a lot of time misunderstanding each other."

Her breath went still. "Sometimes it's better not to try and understand. Sometimes it's better just to take things at face value."

He reached out and ran his finger along her jaw. "What's the market on face value these days?"

She knew she should stop him, but she couldn't. She didn't want to.

He touched his lips to hers and every nerve in her body sparked. In that instant, she became powerless against her own long-dormant desire.

He cupped her face in his hands and kissed her hungrily. Her heart pounded so hard she could feel it from her stomach to her throat. She wanted this. God, she wanted this. But she knew she shouldn't. It was wrong, there was too much water under this bridge. But wrong didn't matter. All that mattered was the feel of Nicholas's lips against hers, the smell of him, the taste of him.

He pulled her closer and soon they were like teenagers in the back seat of a Chevy, without conscience, without control. It was dizzying. Megan felt a sizzle run straight down the core of her body, begging her to keep going. Time stood still. Or perhaps it raced backward, it was hard to say. She hadn't felt this kind of desire in as long as she could remember.

She hadn't felt it in eleven years.

That thought sobered her quickly. This wasn't what she was here for. She and Nicholas couldn't become involved again, especially not like this. Obviously this was just a manifestation of old feelings they'd never fully dismissed. It wasn't about now.

Megan drew back. "We can't."

He trailed his finger down her cheek. "Why not?"

"You know why not. We can't get involved like this. It's unprofessional." She scrambled for something, anything, to erase the last two minutes. "It's—it's wrong."

"It's not wrong," he scoffed. "We're not living in some Victorian novel."

"I can't get involved with you that way, Nicholas," she said evenly, returning to her seat and, hopefully, her composure. "We ended it once. Let's just let it stay ended, okay?"

He raised a questioning brow but gave a single nod.

Several minutes passed in uncomfortable silence.

"I understand your marriage to Jennifer didn't work out," Megan said, instantly regretting bringing up the subject. But she couldn't think of her romantic relationship with Nicholas without thinking of the reason it ended.

"These things happen," he said vaguely. She thought it was a rebuff until he added, "In hindsight, the marriage didn't really stand much of a chance."

Her heart rate increased. "Why not?"

He hesitated long enough for her to anticipate what was coming next.

"Our interests were too different for us to live together."

Megan felt her whole body deflate. Well, what had she expected? For him to say his marriage had failed because he was in love with her?

"We were never in the same place at the same time," he concluded.

"In America I think that's what's known as irreconcilable differences," Megan said softly.

"It's a fair assessment." He set his champagne glass down on a shelf that appeared to be made just for that purpose. "No regrets, though. Everything worked out as planned, regardless. Our families were satisfied. No harm done."

She longed to correct him, to throw the truth in his face like the glass of champagne he'd just set aside.

Her anger surprised her. She thought she'd reached a point of peace where her failed relationship with Nicholas was concerned. It was past.

William, she reminded herself. *William is the only one who matters now.*

"All's well that ends well." The tired old expression was the only thing that came to her. After that kiss, she was lucky any words at all were coming to her.

He nodded, giving away nothing with his expression.

She looked out the window at the crowded London street. Lots of people, probably tourists, turned to look as the big car passed. Megan leaned back against the soft seat and tried to allow herself to enjoy it, but his 'no harm done' comment continued to anger her.

"I'm afraid the dinner might be somewhat tedious," he said as the car slowed in the congested traffic of the West End. "We really only need to make a token appearance. If you'd prefer not to stay, we don't have to."

She looked at him sharply. "Are you having second thoughts about bringing me?"

"No," he said sincerely. "But I'm afraid you may have second thoughts about coming in a moment."

"What do you mean?"

The car drew to a halt outside the theater and this time Nicholas stayed in place, allowing the driver to come around and open the door.

"There's a bit of excitement here, so smile," he said dryly as the door opened. "Keep walking. It will be over in just a moment."

"What on earth are you talking about?" She took the hand the driver proffered and stepped out onto a red carpet she hadn't noticed before. Flashbulbs began to pop from all directions. Before she could register confusion, Nicholas was at her side, his hand large and strong on her upper arm, steadying her as they made their way to the safety of the lobby.

It felt like an amusement park ride.

"What was *that* all about?" Megan asked breathlessly when they got inside, allowing herself a quick glance back at the sea of photographers behind them. One more flash popped, and she turned back to Nicholas.

"Nigel has proclaimed this to be his last play, so they're making it into a big event." He was utterly unfazed, which led her to realize that perhaps this kind of media interest wasn't entirely foreign to him.

"It must be difficult to be in the spotlight all the time." As they walked, Megan drank in the opulence of the theater, the crystal chandeliers, the hush of voices, the light tinkling of wineglasses. It was like a dream or a fairy tale.

She tried to forget Prince Charming's kiss.

"I'm sorry," he said earnestly. "I know how you hate this kind of thing."

Hate it? She didn't. In fact, she was actually rather liking it. She caught a glimpse of one of the latest Hollywood action heroes, standing beside last year's It Girl and felt like she was in Madame Tussaud's Wax Museum. "I've never even experienced this kind of thing."

"I mean on principle. You used to rail on against all the attention and privilege given to people who were born into their luck.'' He looked at her and cocked his sensual mouth into a half smile. ''Have you changed your mind about that?''

Had she? Had she ever really felt that strongly about it? ''I've changed a lot of things in the last nearly eleven years. I was just a young girl then.''

''Not that young.''

''No,'' she had to agree. She'd been old enough to become a mother. ''But young enough to have a lot of opinions without a lot of evidence to support them.''

''Nicholas!'' a woman's voice called. Megan recognized an American television actress coming toward them with her arms extended. ''Nicholas Chapman, what a shock to see you here. We were all talking about you earlier and no one thought you'd actually come tonight.''

Megan couldn't help smiling. The woman had been Nurse Judy Lindon on a hospital TV series in the late 1980s, then had done a couple of shampoo commercials before dropping off the radar. Megan couldn't believe she was standing in front of her now.

''I didn't want to miss Nigel's last performance,'' Nicholas said, then gestured toward Megan. ''Megan Stewart, this is Dana Rappaport.''

''It's nice to meet you,'' Megan said, extending a hand.

''Why, you're American!'' Her hand was warm but her tone had a chill edge to it.

''Yes.''

''I always heard Nicholas preferred American girls.

Apart from one bad experience, that is.'' She winked at him in a way that seemed more lewd than warm and perky. "Back before he got married.''

Megan's stomach lurched. "Really?'' She didn't know what else to say. She looked at him, wondering who or what the one bad experience Dana referred to was. Had he dated another American? Perhaps a whole line of them? Had she been the start of some sort of fetish for him? The whole subject made her extremely uneasy.

It obviously made him uneasy too, because he cleared his throat and looked at his watch. "We'd better take our seats now. Dana, it was good to see you.''

"And you, sweetie, don't be a stranger.''

"Nice meeting you,'' Megan said feebly as they walked away. When they were out of earshot she said to Nicholas, "Have you dated many American girls?''

"No.'' His voice was controlled.

"But she just said—''

"She doesn't know what she's talking about.''

"She seemed quite specific.''

"She's a gossip, dealing in half-truths.'' His tone was brusque.

"Well, where did she get half the truth?'' Megan persisted. "Did you tell her?''

"I knew her ex-husband. I suppose he told her something and she mangled it.''

They arrived at their seats and sat uncomfortably on faded silk. Megan wanted to ask more, to find out

what Dana had been referring to, but the lights went
down and a hush fell over the audience and the theater
demanded she hold her peace.

Megan sat in the dark, her mind racing with
thoughts of their kiss and memories of their past, and
a horrible tape repeating Dana's words over and over,
saying Nicholas had had a bad experience with an
American.

Megan wasn't jealous, she told herself. It just made
her extremely uncomfortable to think that there had
been other American girls. If Dana had said he'd
dated fifteen hundred British women it wouldn't have
been nearly as discomfiting.

On the other hand, what if Megan herself was the
bad experience Dana referred to? It wasn't out of the
question, considering that they *had* dated just prior to
his marriage.

Still, the idea was unthinkable. How had it been
bad for him? All he'd done was play with Megan for
a few months, then drop her like a hot potato. While
the experience had been loaded for her, it was really
quite simple for him.

Could he really have considered their time together
such a big mistake that he actually confided that to
friends? If so, how could she go on to tell him that
the mistake was bigger than he thought?

And how could she let William into a situation like
that?

Leave it to that damn Dana Rappaport to open her
mouth, Nicholas thought bitterly during the play. Not

to mention that louse of an ex-husband of hers, Ben Zaharis. Obviously Nicholas had said too much to Ben and he knew exactly when. They'd been drinking and playing darts in a bar a couple of months after Nicholas and Jennifer had announced their engagement. In fact, it was the night he'd gotten Megan's letter. Nicholas and Ben had burned through almost a whole bottle of Beefeaters gin.

For one drunken moment that night in the pub, he'd actually decided to drive to Heathrow and catch the next plane to the U.S., everything else be damned. Ben had talked him out of it, which in retrospect had been very fortunate, but he'd obviously gone on to spread the tale so well that it endured ten years later.

It was painfully obvious that Dana's statement had upset Megan. His first impulse was to explain to her, but his explanation could only have made things worse. For one thing, it would have confirmed her suspicion that Dana was talking about her. For another it would have opened a wound that had long since closed.

Sitting in the dark, trying to pay attention to Henry Higgins and Eliza Doolittle on stage, Nicholas could only dwell on it.

After what seemed an eternity, the play ended and they gathered their things in silence and went out into the lobby.

"Pendragons is across the street," Nicholas said, half wondering if Megan would just call it a night. "We're to meet everyone there."

"Fine," Megan said, with a tense smile. "I'm looking forward to it."

He didn't believe the smile or the sentiment. In fact, she sounded as ill at ease as he felt. Only a fool would miss the fact that her mood, and his, had altered following their encounter with Dana.

They spoke simultaneously.

"Look, about Dana Rappaport—"

"I have to ask you—"

They stopped.

Megan was the first to say, "Go on."

He tried again, annoyed with the awkwardness he was suddenly feeling. It wasn't as if he was inexperienced with women—why did every contact with Megan make him feel as if he was? "I just hope you weren't upset by what Dana Rappaport said earlier."

"I was confused by it," she answered, but before she could finish, they were interrupted by a reporter for *On the Town* magazine.

"Earl Shrafton, how was the show?" he asked, after flashing his credentials.

"Excellent," Nicholas answered stiffly. He wanted to put an arm around Megan and usher her quickly away from the reporter, but he knew she would stiffen at his touch, and he didn't want to feel that. "I recommend it highly."

"Will you be joining Sir Nigel's party now at…?"

"Excuse us," Nicholas said, going ahead and taking Megan's arm to protect her from the intrusion. To his surprise, she didn't stiffen. She stepped closer. Every nerve in his body charged.

They continued walking through the lobby with the reporter close behind, but suddenly Nicholas didn't mind quite so much.

"May I have your name, Miss?" the man asked, holding up his pad and poised pen.

"Megan," she answered, with an uncertain glance at Nicholas.

He smiled. "Answer at your own risk," he said softly.

"And are you the earl's latest fancy?"

Her stomach twisted in a knot as she thought again of the kiss in the limo. Thank goodness she'd stopped it when she did. "No, I'm not."

Nicholas tightened his grip on her arm and they picked up the pace, leaving the single reporter in the lobby for a sea of photographers and reporters outside. The flashes popped and a couple of voices called "Earl!" or "Nick!" as they hurried past, but there were stage and film stars of varying levels of fame behind them and the attention was quickly diverted.

They went down a block and crossed the street, then turned up a sleepy corridor where Pendragons was located in a building that was at least two hundred years old. As soon as they walked in, they were escorted to a private room in the back, where several people Megan recognized, including Sir Nigel, already were.

"Nicholas!" the older actor called, coming over to give Nicholas a hearty pat on the back. "So good to see you, my boy." He turned his famous eyes to Megan and smiled. "Who have we here?"

"This is Megan Stewart, an old friend of mine," Nicholas said. "Megan, this is Nigel Drake."

"Megan, what a pleasure to meet you." Nigel kissed her hand. "Why does that name sound familiar?"

"Didn't you play a character named Stewart in one of your films?" Nicholas asked quickly.

Nigel gave him a mock severe look. "I never confuse work and reality, my boy," he said with an ironic smile. "Although I threaten to more as the years pass." He turned back to Megan. "Are you certain we've never met before?"

"Absolutely certain."

"Ah, well," he said, waving a gnarled hand. "It will come to me. Tell me, did you enjoy the show?"

"Very much," Megan effused. "I've always loved the story, but you brought something to the role of Henry Higgins that made it even better than usual."

"Age," Nigel said, frowning. "That's what the papers said, that I was too old for the role." He laughed and several people turned to look. "I daresay they're right. But to hell with them anyway, eh?"

Megan laughed. "To hell with them," she agreed. "I thought you were marvelous."

She looked so lovely that Nicholas felt proud to be with her.

"I like you," Nigel said, smiling from her to Nicholas and back. "If we haven't met before, we should have. Any road up, I'm glad to see Nicholas getting out some, and with such a charming lady. He's spent far too much time working these past few years."

"Let's not get into that again," Nicholas said, trying to stop the conversation.

"He never wants to talk about his private life," Nigel said to Megan conspiratorially. "Makes for such dull conversation, really. Maybe you're the one to change that, dear girl." He winked at Nicholas.

Megan's face turned pink.

"Don't you go putting her on the spot," Nicholas said, trying to avert her embarrassment. "She's just a friend, don't go making it into something else."

"Then you're a fool, my boy." Nigel laughed loudly. "Why if I was twenty or thirty years younger I'd be trying to court her myself." The smile he gave Megan was kind. "You remind me of the great love of my life, Rita Hayworth. Has anyone ever told you that before?"

She shook her head. "No one's ever told me I looked like Rita Hayworth *or* the love of their life, so thank you very much for both compliments."

An objection rose in Nicholas's chest.

"Which raises an interesting question," Nigel said. "Who was the love of *your* life, my dear? At least so far."

Megan looked stunned for an instant. "The love of *my* life?"

"Mm-hmm."

Nicholas waited, simultaneously hating the question and wanting to know her answer.

After a time of consideration, Megan said quietly, "I guess I'd have to say it was my son's father."

Nicholas expelled a breath he hadn't realized he'd been holding.

"I assume, from the way you say that, you're no longer with the man," Nigel said, delving into her personal life with that incredible gall he'd always had.

"No." She shook her head. "No, I'm not."

Nigel raised his gaze to Nicholas. "I'm not even going to ask you the same question." He looked at Megan. "I've known this boy all his life and have never known him to let his emotions get the better of him. Pity, really."

Eager to stop this uncomfortable conversation at almost any cost, Nicholas was about to bring up the damp weather they'd been having, when across the room people started clinking their glasses and calling for a speech from Nigel.

It didn't take a great deal of persuasion. "Dear friends," he said, with a grand sweep of his hand, "both old and new," a quick nod at Megan, "I am so grateful you have all joined me tonight on this, my final opening night. Mine has been a wonderful life. Remember that if the critics kill me with the morning notices." Laughter waved across the crowd.

"And remember one more thing." He looked at Nicholas. "This champagne is nice and so is the waiter who brought it to me, but in the end all that matters is love. Without it, everything else is ultimately meaningless." He raised his glass then drank.

Everyone in the room followed suit except Nicholas, who felt frozen where he stood.

At that moment, Dana Rappaport reappeared and

◄ **DETACH AND MAIL CARD TODAY!** ▶

YES!

I have scratched off the silver card. Please send me the 2 FREE books and gift for which I qualify. I understand I am under no obligation to purchase any books, as explained on the back and on the opposite page.

With a coin, scratch off the silver card and check below to see what we have for you.

SILHOUETTE'S

LUCKY HEARTS GAME

315 SDL C6QQ

215 SDL C6QL
(S-R-OS-07/01)

NAME   (PLEASE PRINT CLEARLY)

ADDRESS

APT.#   CITY

STATE/PROV.   ZIP/POSTAL CODE

Twenty-one gets you 2 free books, and a free mystery gift!

Twenty gets you 2 free books!

Nineteen gets you 1 free book!

Try Again!

The Silhouette Reader Service™—Here's how it works:

Accepting your 2 free books and gift places you under no obligation to buy anything. You may keep the books and gift and return the shipping statement marked "cancel." If you do not cancel, about a month later we'll send you 6 additional novels and bill you just $2.90 each in the U.S., or $3.25 each in Canada, plus 25¢ shipping & handling per book and applicable taxes if any.* That's the complete price and — compared to cover prices of $3.50 each in the U.S. and $3.99 each in Canada — it's quite a bargain! You may cancel at any time, but if you choose to continue, every month we'll send you 6 more books, which you may either purchase at the discount price or return to us and cancel your subscription.

*Terms and prices subject to change without notice. Sales tax applicable in N.Y. Canadian residents will be charged applicable provincial taxes and GST.

If offer card is missing write to: Silhouette Reader Service, 3010 Walden Ave., P.O. Box 1867, Buffalo, NY 14240-1867

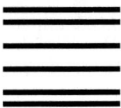

BUSINESS REPLY MAIL

FIRST-CLASS MAIL   PERMIT NO. 717   BUFFALO, NY

POSTAGE WILL BE PAID BY ADDRESSEE

SILHOUETTE READER SERVICE
3010 WALDEN AVE
PO BOX 1867
BUFFALO NY 14240-9952

NO POSTAGE
NECESSARY
IF MAILED
IN THE
UNITED STATES

took Megan by the arm. "Meg, you just have to come see my friend Glenda, she's *dying* to meet you!"

Megan threw a glance back at Nicholas, who watched helplessly as she was led away to God-knew-what kind of gossip.

"What's the matter, dear boy?" Nigel asked, all innocence.

"Nothing at all," Nicholas said, then hastily sipped from his glass. He glanced at Megan, but looked away quickly when he caught her puzzled gaze. "I have an important meeting tomorrow and I'm afraid I'm having a hard time keeping my mind off it."

"Trouble at work, eh?" Nigel asked, raising an eyebrow so dramatically it was almost comical.

"It never ends."

"It's fortunate that you're successful in your career," he said, lazily sipping from his glass. "Because you'll never be an actor."

Nicholas felt the blood drain from his face. "I'm not sure what you mean."

"I mean you're crazy about that girl," the older man said. "And you're terrible at hiding it. Honestly, I thought you'd have learned a little something about having a poker face from me by now."

Nicholas gave his best smile and shook his head. "You're wrong this time, old fellow."

Nigel raised his brow. "Am I? I don't think so. As a matter of fact, I believe I remember where I've heard her name before."

"I'm certain you haven't heard her name before."

"You were involved with her years ago, weren't you? Your parents were most concerned."

"They needn't have been. I kept up my end of the deal."

"Mmm, yes, you did." Nigel's face registered disapproval. "For better or worse. It's as I said, you've never allowed your emotions to get the better of you. You don't know what you've missed. I hope you won't make that same mistake again."

"I didn't make a mistake."

"Just like your father, you never admit when you're wrong."

"I did the right thing."

"You keep saying it and someone might believe you." Nigel took an extravagant draw from his glass. "Not me, of course, but someone."

"Can we change the subject?"

"Certainly. We can discuss whatever you like. But first," he lowered his voice and touched his finger to the corner of his mouth, "you have a bit of lipstick just there."

Nicholas felt his face grow hot as he took out his handkerchief and swiped it across his mouth. "Gone?"

Nigel nodded sagely. "Far gone, I'd say."

Nicholas shook his head, then watched Megan across the room with Dana and her party for a couple of seconds before saying, "I think I'd better go rescue Megan from the sharks."

Nigel followed his gaze. "Yes, I see what you mean."

"Excuse me." Nicholas crossed the room just as Megan was extricating herself from the group. "Everything all right?" he asked when he got to her.

She had grown slightly pale. "I'd like to go home now," she said quietly.

"What happened?"

When she looked at him, he felt as if he'd been struck. Her voice was icy, but he knew some angry flame had been reignited. "I want to go home," she repeated. "Please."

It had been a long time since he'd known Megan, but not so long that he didn't recognize when she was in pain. "Fine," he said. "I'll just tell Nigel—"

"I'll see myself out," she said, not waiting for him to finish. "I can get home on my own."

"Megan—"

She didn't wait to hear him out, but started toward the door so quickly he had to choose between good manners—telling Nigel he was leaving—and rushing after Megan, to find out what was wrong and what he could do to make it better.

He chose Megan.

Chapter Seven

"**Y**ou look upset," Nicholas said, unable to follow up with anything helpful. Of course she was upset. He himself had heard enough to explain why.

"I'm fine." She looked at her wrist, where a watch should have been but wasn't. "But it's getting late and I have to go."

He knew a ticking time bomb when he saw one. There would be no arguing with her about going back inside, no persuading her to forget Dana and whatever she'd said. The only thing he could do was respect her wish and take her home.

They walked a couple of blocks without speaking. The streets were busy and noisy, but Megan's silence was still noticeable. Finally, though he didn't want to give any credence to Dana Rappaport and her gossip, he had to ask, "What did Dana say this time?"

Megan stopped in front of the tube station and looked him hard in the eye. "She said enough."

"That's not really an answer."

"She said your American girlfriend was a big joke in your set."

"Then she lied."

Megan ran a hand through her hair, looked into distance and heaved a sigh, before looking back at Nicholas. "I know I don't have the right to ask but I have to anyway, when Dana said that one American you dated had been a 'big mistake,' who was she referring to?"

He took a deep breath. Of course he'd known this was coming. "There's nothing I can say to make this okay with you. If I say it was you, you'll feel bad, and if I tell you there was a line of American girls standing behind you when you left, you'll feel bad about that too."

She didn't meet his eyes. "You're right."

He shrugged. "I don't know what to say."

Now she did meet his eyes. "How about the truth? Don't try to play the angles like this is some kind of touchy business deal, just tell me the truth."

He didn't cower from her gaze, but sent it right back to her. "All right, she was referring to you."

Her face paled. "She was."

"Rather, *I* was referring to you when I spoke too freely to her hen of a husband a decade ago. Her retaining the information, much less happening to regurgitate it the very moment you and I go out together, is just obscenely bad luck."

She looked so hurt his heart ached.

"Was I really a 'bad experience' to you?" she asked, practically whispering.

Nicholas hesitated. "You have to admit, it didn't end well."

But it had begun well, he couldn't help thinking. Memories came to him like movie clips before the main feature. Those first lingering kisses on Waterloo Bridge; the first tentative touches, exploring each other's bodies; the long nights spent in bed in his Kensington flat, gazing out the window at the sky, talking until the sun began to rise in the distance...

"I know it ended badly." Megan's voice was steady. "Believe me, I'm well aware of how it ended. But even so, I didn't come away from it thinking the whole relationship was a bad experience. I didn't regret the time we spent together." She blinked fast and slipped her hand across her eyes. A taxi swooshed past and she watched it. "And maybe I was foolish, but I never thought you might have regretted it."

"Realizing it was a mistake and regretting it are not exactly the same thing," Nicholas said, evading the bigger point. Did he regret it? Considering how painful it had been to end it, he thought perhaps he did. It would have been easier to have never loved her. "Besides, it was my mistake, not yours."

She gaped at him. "I beg your pardon?"

He never had this much trouble expressing himself. "What I mean is, I take full responsibility for the way everything went." How could he blame her for being so beautiful that he couldn't resist her? "I knew I couldn't follow through but..." He let out a long breath and looked at her. The truth was, she was more beautiful now than she had been ten years ago. Temptation could be more of an issue now than ever before. Thank goodness he was stronger now than he had been then. "It was my responsibility," he repeated. "I'm sorry. But, really, does any of this matter now? We should wipe the slate clean."

"Easier said than done," she replied, looking at him with a directness he didn't often see.

"The alternative is that we avoid each other entirely. I'm not accustomed to living my life that way."

"Well, it is all about what *you're* comfortable with, isn't it?" She started walking into the station. "Nothing's changed there."

"That's not fair."

She stopped and turned back. "*Life* isn't always fair, Nicholas," she said angrily. "You don't always have the luxury of having things go according to your plans and desires."

"I'm well aware of that."

Her eyes grew fiery. "No, no, I don't mean your stocks don't always sell for as much as you want them to, or that every once in awhile your favorite limo driver is ill and you have to use another. I mean sometimes life throws real curveballs at you and you just have to adapt. You can't simply 'wipe the slate clean' and pretend they didn't happen."

"Megan." He took her by the arm.

She wrenched it free. She would not let him turn her to mush with his touch, not this time. "What?"

"Don't overreact."

"*Overreact?* I'm sorry, is this uncomfortable for you? Don't you like hearing the truth?"

"The *truth,*" he said, overly patient, "is that a long time ago we knew each other for a short time." He gave her the speech he'd given himself a hundred times over the years. He'd never believed it but maybe she would and they'd both be the better for it. "It was fun while it lasted but it wasn't real life. Let's let it be a pleasant memory and go on from there, all right?"

She looked at him with something that appeared to be contempt, then said in an icy tone. "You're right. And if you'll forgive me, I think I'd better go home to my *real* life."

Never in his life had he been with someone who could make him feel like such a bumbling idiot. "Of course, if that's what you want, but—"

"It's what I want."

"I'll call for the car," he said, taking a slim mobile phone from his pocket.

"Don't bother. I'll take the tube." She held up a hand to stop his objections. "Goodnight, Nicholas." With that, she disappeared into the station.

"Is it true that Lord Byron killed his mistress and now she is the white lady who haunts the abbey?"

Megan looked at her student with surprise. The young man appeared completely earnest in his query.

"I don't think that's true," she said, considering the possibility for a moment. "The English aristocracy does have a rich history of getting rid of inconvenient wives and mistresses." The grim irony did not escape her. "But they also have a rigid justice system. If Lord Byron had killed his mistress, it would probably be a matter of official record." She smiled. "It makes a great story, but I don't think it's true."

"It wouldn't have to be recorded. Not if he killed her and buried her behind a wall or something," someone called out.

"Like the twins in the tower!"

Megan was about to call out for control when, mercifully, the bell rang. "I hope you'll all read the Washington Irving piece on Abbotsford and Newstead Abbey before we go next week."

There was a general murmur of assent as the students piled their books and clopped out of the classroom, smiling and nodding at her on their way past.

"Ms. Stewart?"

Megan looked up from her papers to see Suzanne Hart, a shy girl of about eighteen years old, standing before her, kneading her hands.

"You don't need to be so formal. Call me Megan."

Suzanne ran a hand through her long dark chestnut hair. "Okay." She blushed, then cleared her throat. "I wanted to ask about the trip to Nottingham. Does everyone have to go or is it optional?"

Megan furrowed her brow. "Nothing is mandatory but I'd hate to see you miss a great opportunity." She studied the girl. "And your grades could suffer if you don't keep up with the class. Are you saying you'd rather not join us on the trip?''

"It's not that I'm not interested or anything, it's just..." Something at the door caught the girl's eye. She gave a weak smile, then turned back to Megan. "Never mind. I was just wondering." Her eyes flitted nervously to the door again.

Megan followed the girl's gaze and her heart nearly stopped when she saw Nicholas standing there, looking startlingly handsome in an ash-grey pinstripe suit. Every dark blond hair was in place but his smile was, as it had always been, suggestive that he was harboring rakish thoughts on the inside.

It had been two weeks since Megan had seen him last and she had begun to think that she had made a huge mistake in letting Dana's comments get to her. So what if he regretted his relationship with Megan? Okay, it was a hurtful thing to hear, but it didn't change the facts.

These days Megan had to deal in facts, not feelings.

So she was glad to see him. It saved her the embarrassment of having to go to him and gloss over what had happened after the play.

"Hello, Megan," he said, as casually as if they had just run into each other on a pleasant afternoon in the park.

"Hi," Megan returned, her voice sounding thin and strained.

Suzanne seemed to sense the tension. "Excuse me," she said, going back to her desk and gathering her books. "I'll see you this Friday Ms. Stew— Megan."

Somehow Megan managed to return her smile. "Good. Seven o'clock at Kings Cross Station."

When they were alone, Megan turned back to Nicholas. "This is a surprise." Damn the rapid pounding of her heart. It was going to give her away; her face was probably crimson.

"I came to call a truce. Again." He smiled that pirate smile again. "Hopefully it will take this time."

There was no point in being coy and pretending they didn't have a problem. "Good idea."

He didn't just turn and leave, of course. "Will you have lunch with me?"

Why did the idea of spending more time alone with him make her feel so afraid? The answer came to her in the form of a memory. A memory of the kiss they'd shared in the back of the limo, and of the intense desire she'd felt for him. And of the near inability to stop things once they started.

"I have a class coming up." Her next class was an hour and fifteen minutes away.

"At one o'clock," Nicholas said smoothly.

"How did—" She narrowed her eyes. "I gather that your involvement with the program allows you access to all sorts of information."

"Right." He didn't appear in the least embarrassed. "You have no secrets."

That comment landed with a thud. Megan busied herself straightening the already-straight papers on her desk. "Well, I appreciate the offer but I have to prepare for my next class and that's going to take awhile. Maybe some other time.'' She tried to go around him but he stepped in her path.

''Megan, this awkwardness has to stop.'' He took a breath, as if to say more, but only expelled it.

''I agree.'' She took a short breath. ''I wish I knew how because we have much more important things to deal with.'' The words were out before she stopped to think. Their eyes met. Megan looked immediately away.

''Like what?''

''Classes,'' she bluffed. ''In fact, as you're probably aware, I'm taking one to your estate for a visit this weekend.'' She tried to assume a look of nonchalance. ''Are you going to be there?''

To her great relief, he shook his head. ''I'm glad to let the students go and poke around but I don't particularly relish the idea of being in the middle of it. The staff will take care of you.''

''I didn't mean to suggest we needed you there to take care of us,'' Megan said, honestly trying to assure him that she didn't want to take advantage.

He took it the wrong way. ''No, you wouldn't want that, you've made that clear.'' His expression hardened. ''I can't get anywhere with you. No matter what I say, you take the opposite stance. If I say black, you say white.''

''That's not true!''

''Yes, it is. Either it's me or it's the whole damn world you're angry with.'' He cocked the corner of his mouth into an ironic half-smile. ''I think it's me.''

Her heart pounded but a tiny voice within told her it was true. She was so defensive with him that she wouldn't have accepted water from him if she was dying of thirst in the desert.

"You used to be different," he said, in a tone that was both angry and perhaps a little sad.

"Yes," she said defiantly. "Life used to be a lot simpler."

He leaned against the desk and studied her. "Is life really so damned hard now?"

"Not for you, apparently."

"Look, I realize that a lot of things have changed—"

"I'll say."

His mouth tightened. "This was a mistake." He turned to go. If she didn't stop him, he would be gone. Then there might not be another chance to tell him the truth.

There might not be another chance to fix everything that was wrong.

He was almost in the hall when she said it. "Nicky."

He stopped.

The word hung in the air between them.

That she said it surprised her as much as it did him. It had been almost eleven years since she'd called him that, or really thought of him that way. She hadn't meant to say it now, but there it was. Her hands flexed at her sides.

What was she going to say now?

He turned. Silence pulsed between them. She was

suddenly aware of a strong pull toward him. She wanted to run into his arms, to bury her face in his powerful chest and let everything else—all these emotions that ripped through her—fall away. He was always able to make things better for her. When she'd felt homesick, he'd been able to cheer her with a small joke or well-placed kiss. When she'd felt anxious, he'd always been able to soothe her with a touch. And when she'd had a problem, he'd always been able to see a clear and logical answer to take care of it.

Megan forced herself to look away. Back down at the desk. "I'm not the only one who's changed."

"No?" He took three steady steps toward her. "How have I changed?"

"You have this—this wall you've put up between you and the rest of the world. Like nothing surprises you. Like nothing touches you. You're above it all."

"You would prefer that I walk the streets weeping copiously?"

She held her hands up. "It's none of my business. I shouldn't have said a thing."

"But you did."

"Forget it."

"Until the next time you hint at it? Until the next time we have a strained meeting that ends with one of us walking away with some throwaway line tossed over the shoulder?"

"You're right. It seems inevitable. Maybe we *should* just avoid each other." She realized the problem with that only after she said it. "Except we can't.'' She looked into his eyes, searching for the old Nicholas she'd felt she connected so well with. "We have unfinished business." She searched his face, seeing the familiar and the unfamiliar in every feature. She could no longer tell what she recognized of the boy she remembered from what she recognized in his son. "We need to talk it out."

His gaze lingered on her. Finally he spoke. "There's a terrible cafeteria in this building where they have weak tea, stale scones and cold Scotch eggs. I thought I'd go for a cup of coffee, would you join me? Please."

After the merest hesitation, she nodded. "But I don't have long."

It wouldn't take long to say what she had to. How long it would take to live through the repercussions, though, she couldn't guess.

They took a small squeaky elevator up to the top floor. As it jerked along its course, Megan thought several times that it might stop or go crashing down, and that she might be glad if it did. It arrived safely, though, and five minutes later the two of them had loaded a tray with coffee, scones and packets of butter, and stepped out of the cafeteria onto the rooftop picnic area.

It was a very ordinary place to break the extraordinary news to him.

The metal table was right next to an enormous air vent but the view in the opposite direction was lovely. Jagged rooftops speared toward the sky, and there were snatches of green parkland between them. A warm September breeze carried the distinct scents of diesel fuel, drying leaves and the last summer flowers.

Megan turned her face toward the sunlight and closed her eyes. For just a moment, she felt like the girl she used to be. With the boy she used to love. She wished she could hold on to that feeling, but she knew that in a few minutes it would all come tumbling down.

"Where should we start?" Nicholas asked. "With your life or mine?"

"Yours." Her hands trembled so much that she didn't dare pick up her cup. "Tell me what you do for a living these days," she said, buying a little bit of time.

He did. He told her about the frustration he felt in his father's business, and the resolve he had finally reached to leave it and start his own ventures. He told her about several of the more rewarding aspects of his enterprises, and he told her that London Study was one of his favorites.

"How did you happen to become involved?" she asked, wondering if it had anything to do with her, or if it was vain of her to even suspect it. "I mean, did you initiate it or just take on a figurehead role to help them out?"

He looked pained. "I'm not just a figurehead."

She was immediately sorry. "What I meant was, did they approach you?"

He shook his head. "It existed before I ever came along, though not exactly in its present form. I heard about this organization that helped financially underprivileged kids, kids who wouldn't otherwise be able to take a trip to the next state, take a semester here and I thought it was a worthy cause." He grew silent for a moment and his jaw tensed.

"It's a good program." She gave half a smile but felt every word they said was loaded. "My time here in college changed my life." Their eyes met.

She realized, in the space of that small moment, that it didn't matter how she had gotten where she had, because she was happy with it. It didn't matter what the circumstances were surrounding William's existence, she was just so glad to have him.

She looked at him evenly. "I wouldn't trade it for anything."

"I'm glad to hear it. I—" He hesitated and looked out over the landscape. "I thought about you sometimes. Quite a bit, in fact." He cleared his throat. "I worried about you, I'm afraid. You were so upset when you left."

"Yes."

His voice softened. "I'm sorry I hurt you." He didn't touch her but he may as well have.

Megan, who was in the process of buttering a scone to keep her hands busy, stopped, but didn't meet his eyes. "That doesn't matter anymore."

He shrugged. "If it didn't, we wouldn't argue every time we see each other, would we?"

She took a deep breath. "It's not as simple as you think," she said unsteadily.

"What do you mean?"

"It didn't end with me leaving." She swallowed hard. "After I got home—"

"Ms. Stewart?"

Megan's shoulders dropped. She felt like dough that had just risen, only to be punched down again. One of her students was coming toward her with a scone in hand and jam smeared across his cheek.

She'd never been so irritated by an interruption.

He loped over like a puppy, oblivious to the glare Megan gave him. "Uh, Ms. Stewart, I was wondering about this trip we're supposed to take?"

She waited. "Yes? What about it?"

"Well, um, are we staying overnight or what?"

She collected herself. He didn't know what he was doing, he was just asking his teacher a question. "Yes, I'm in the process of making arrangements with an inn in the center of town."

"Oh." He remained standing in front of them.

"Was there anything else?" she asked, just a tad impatiently.

He looked from her to Nicholas and gave a goofy smile. "Oh. Sorry. Yeah, I was wondering, are the rooms, you know, co-ed?"

"No." She narrowed her eyes. "In fact, you'll be sharing four to a room."

"Bummer."

She gave a small smile, hoping he'd get the hint and leave. "Is that all you wanted to know?"

"Uh, yeah, I guess so." He took another bite, smearing even more jam on his face in the process, then waved with the scone. "See ya Friday."

She watched him go and sighed. "They're so much younger now than when I was that age."

Nicholas laughed. "I know what you mean. Were we ever so coarse?"

She looked back at him. "You never were." She allowed herself a moment's indulgence in remembrance. Nicholas had been smart and funny, but he'd also had a very fluid social grace. She couldn't imagine that he'd ever been a jam-smeared, tongue-tied teenager. "Most of my students aren't like that."

Nicholas tapped his fingers on the table. "Megan, why don't you and the students stay at my place in Nottingham instead of trying to squeeze into some cheap hotel?"

"Who says it's a cheap hotel?"

"The budget. I've looked it over a hundred times over the years." He leaned back. "I've got a hundred and forty-four rooms that are currently unoccupied. Perhaps it would be more comfortable for you and more interesting for your students."

For a moment she was tempted to accept but then she thought better of it and shook her head. "I don't think it's a very good idea. You don't know what these kids are like. The place would be in a shambles after an hour." She lifted her cup of tea to her lips to try and calm the shaking that had begun when she'd nearly told him about William.

Nicholas persisted. "It's stood for six hundred years, and through more wars and battles than I could count. I think it could survive a night of college kids."

She set the cup down. "No, thanks. I couldn't impose." She glanced at the clock on the wall and realized her chance with Nicholas had gone, at least this time. "Good Lord, I only have fifteen minutes before my next class." So much for her plans. "I appreciate your offer, Nicholas. It was very kind."

"Listen," he said, pulling a gold box out of his breast pocket. "Go ahead and try to make other arrangements. If you decide you'd like to take me up on this, give me a call." He took out a business card and scribbled on the back. "Here are my home and office numbers." He pressed the card into her hand. "Now I'm afraid we've strayed from the point. You were saying something about after you got home from England?"

Fourteen minutes and counting to her next class time. There was no way she could go into it now. "I've got to go get ready for my next class now. We're going to need to sit down and talk about that uninterrupted sometime," she said. "Are you free, say, tomorrow evening after work?"

He shook his head. "I'm going to Edinburgh tomorrow afternoon. My flight doesn't get in until after ten. And you're going up north on Friday. How about next Monday. Lunch? Dinner? You choose."

"Lunch," she said firmly. The sooner she got this over with, the better. "Lunch on Monday. I'll see you then."

Chapter Eight

Who would have thought that all the suitable accommodations in the Nottingham area would be booked that weekend?

Megan was seated at her kitchen table with a cup of tea, the telephone, a pen and pad and about ten crumpled sheets of paper at her feet. Two things were clear: one was that it would be impossible to do everything she'd planned for the class trip without staying overnight, and the other was that there was nowhere for them to stay.

Except at Nicholas's house.

She reached into her purse, took out the business card he had given her and read it for the hundredth time. It was tempting, very tempting. It would be a wonderful opportunity for the students, staying in one of the Great Houses of Britain. Knowing the stature of Nicholas's family, the ancestral home had probably even been featured on one of those PBS shows. It would be selfish of her to refuse his offer.

She lifted the phone, dialed the first three numbers, then hung up. It would be selfish to refuse, but it was almost impossible to accept. She couldn't imagine going into the house without him there anymore than she could imagine going in *with* him there.

Megan rubbed her hands across her eyes and sighed. There was another factor. She was going to have to take William with her on this trip. If they stayed at Nicholas's ancestral home, they would be staying at William's ancestral home.

Maybe that was a good thing. Since she planned to tell Nicholas the truth on Monday, and presumably would tell William shortly thereafter, it might be a good thing for him to have some familiarity with Nicholas's lifestyle.

It was that idea that decided her.

She took a sip of her hot tea and glanced back down at the hand-scrawled home telephone number on Nicholas's business card.

Then she picked up the phone and dialed.

Nicholas's estate in Nottingham was more glorious than Megan could have imagined. The tree-lined drive wound through what seemed like miles of white birches and gnarled oaks, making Megan feel they were light-years away from the rest of the world. The leaves were changing, and with the sun filtering through, the woods were a luminous burnished gold.

Then, suddenly, the trees fell away to acres of sprawling green lawn, with a massive brick building directly center. This, she could only conclude, was the house, although that word was pitifully small for the structure. It resembled a museum or federal office building more. There must have been a hundred windows facing the front alone. It was easy to imagine a horse-drawn carriage pulling up in the courtyard out front, depositing ornately dressed ladies and gentlemen from centuries past.

She couldn't help but think what a lonely place this must have been for Nicholas as a child. Was it lonely for him still? When he came here now did it look as austere and desolate to him as it did to her? Or did he slip right into the role of Lord of the Manor?

Inside it was even grander, with impossibly high ceilings and gleaming marble floors. Ancient-looking tapestries hung on the walls alongside original oil paintings, including one that, Megan was almost sure, was a Renoir. The furniture was the kind featured in books and magazines on antiques, all of it gleaming like new and completely formidable. It was hardly the sort of thing one would lounge back on while watching the Superbowl playoffs. No, it was much more the sitting-on-the-edge-sipping-tea variety.

Megan couldn't help but picture a young Nicholas here. As beautiful as it was, it had to have been a terrible place for a child. At least, for an only child like Nicholas had been, with parents who were chilly and distant and who never, from what he'd told her so long ago, let laughter ring through the halls.

He had told her once about coming to this estate during his childhood summers, and how only certain rooms had been designated for him to enter. For the most part, he had to keep out of the fussy, antique-filled rooms.

She remembered the story well, because he'd also told her about a patient old gardener who had showed Nicholas how to plant and harvest vegetables. Megan could picture the unlikely pair now, working the earth under a pale English sun. How many of the plants she could see now had young Nicholas's fingerprints on them?

A butler showed them all to their rooms, saving Megan's for last. It was enormous, clearly a master suite. The wide bed had a heavy velvet canopy and bedspread in deep mahogany, matching the drapes. The furniture was heavy and masculine. Megan wondered for a moment if it was Nicholas's room, but dismissed the idea quickly. With so many rooms to pick from, there was no way he'd put her in his private quarters. Nevertheless, she thought she felt something of his presence here.

Then again, she'd been thinking of almost nothing but Nicholas since they'd arrived. Her imagination was probably infusing him into everything she saw, whether it had anything to do with him or not.

William was settled in a smaller room next to hers. Once upon a time it had probably been a baby's nursery, judging from its placement, but it was still about three times the size of his room in London or back home. He loved it.

"Look out the window, Mom!" he cried excitedly. "*Horses!* This guy owns *horses!* Do you think he'd let me ride one?"

"Will, you haven't ridden a horse in years, and even that was at the mini horse farm in Pennsylvania. You wouldn't know what to do with yourself on one of those monsters."

"Yeah, I would, I'd gallop across those big hills out there." His eyes were shining and she knew he was seeing himself crossing the landscape at lighting speed on some magnificent stallion.

"Ease up, cowboy, you're not riding a horse this visit." But, she realized, he might during some visit in the future. The thought of him riding without her around to prevent disaster made her uneasy. She had to get along with Nicholas, if only so that she could stick around during any time they might spend together. Nicholas hadn't been there for the past ten years, preventing catastrophe at every turn, from the stove to the light socket. He would have no conception of how careful he had to be with a child.

"I sure wish we lived here," William said wistfully, leaning his forehead against the windowpane.

She sat down on his bed. "What would you do with a huge place like this?"

He laughed. "You name it. Did you know there's even a pool out back? A *pool,* Mom, and there's no one in it! Can we at least go swimming?"

"That's not what we're here for," she said, then, seeing the disappointment on his face, added, "But maybe, if the pool is in working order and it's warm enough, you can take a quick dip.''

That brightened him up. "All *right*."

"But you'll have to go in your underwear since you didn't bring a swimsuit."

"I brought a swimsuit," he said, jumping up from his place by the window and going to his suitcase.

"You did?" She was amazed. "Why?"

He poked around his clothes, found the suit and turned to her, beaming. "Because we were going away for the weekend. You never know when you're going to stay someplace with a pool."

"No, I guess you don't."

He twirled the suit around his finger, then tossed it back into his case. "I'm going to explore the rest of the house, okay?"

She thought for a moment about any danger he might encounter and decided there probably wasn't any. "Okay, but don't touch anything. There are knickknacks around here that cost more than your whole college education."

"I'll be careful," he called as he trotted out of the room.

Megan straightened his things, and went to her room to unpack. She'd brought along the photo album of William she'd made for Nicholas, intending to make any final notes she'd need to before giving it to him on Monday. She sat for a moment, fingering the faux leather book and thinking how cheap it might seem to someone who lived in an atmosphere like this one. But when she opened it up and saw the pictures of William as a baby in his bouncy seat, William blowing out two candles on his second birthday cake, William in his Scout uniform...she knew there was nothing cheap about it at all.

Carefully she slid the book under some other papers in her briefcase, then decided to take a little walking tour of the house herself. She could hear her students' voices raised in enthusiastic chatter and laughter. What an incredible experience for them, actually staying a night in such a palatial house. Nicholas had been very generous to offer, and Megan was glad she'd taken him up on it, for everyone's sake.

She walked down a hall filled with dark oil portraits of men in waistcoats and women in heavy-looking gowns. These were, presumably, earls and countesses from the past. Nicholas's ancestors.

William's ancestors.

She slowed her pace, studying the faces with intense interest. Some of the earlier ones were done in the old style, long and thin with faces that didn't look quite real. As the years went on, the faces became more and more lifelike, with readable expressions of happiness, detachment or sorrow. The last one she saw stopped her in her tracks. The painted eyes, which appeared to be staring straight at her, looked so much like Nicholas's that it took her breath away. The person in the painting wasn't Nicholas, though. The man's hair was dark, for one thing. Also, his nose was just a little bit straighter and the mouth was set in a thinner line. Still, the eyes were startlingly familiar. It was the first time in over ten years that Megan had been able to just look at them without self-consciousness.

She took a deep breath, aware of an attraction she hadn't allowed herself to feel in ages. It was insane. There was no room in her life for this attraction to Nicholas. That chapter of her life was long over.

Besides, when she told him about William, there was a distinct possibility that he wouldn't even want the most casual of relationships with her.

Which left her to wonder what his relationship with William would be like. Could she really imagine William spending any amount of time in this opulence? It was difficult. His boyish interests were so…normal. He liked Pokémon and his Gameboy, not the history and philosophy that these walls seemed to breathe.

"Ms. Stewart?" The voice that broke through Megan's musings was that of her student, Andrea Pendal.

"Yes, Andrea?" She had grown weary of trying to get her students to call her Megan. It was starting to make her feel like an old woman trying to be hip. She looked at Andrea, and noticed her face was etched with concern.

"Well, I don't know if I should say anything…"

Dread stirred in Megan's breast. Had a Ming vase gone down somewhere? Had someone spilled Coke on a Monet? "What is it?" she asked, an edge sharpening her words.

Andrea bit down on her lower lip. "It's Suzanne. I think she's sick. She's white as a ghost and she barely said two words on the train on the way up."

She shrugged. "Now she won't join the rest of us, she's gone off by herself."

Megan frowned. "Where is she now?"

Andrea kneaded her hands together in front of her. "Outside. She said she needed some fresh air."

"I'll go talk to her." Megan turned to go, then stopped, noticing that the anxiety in the girl's eyes seemed to have deepened. She gave a smile. "Don't look so worried," she assured her. "I'm sure she's just a little homesick or something." But inside she wasn't so sure. Suzanne had been acting somewhat strange for the past few weeks, including missing classes and trying to get out of coming to Nottingham with the group.

When she found Suzanne, the girl was sitting under the shade of an oak by a pond. Megan approached quietly, then cleared her throat to warn Suzanne of her presence.

"Can I join you?" Megan asked when Suzanne turned to see her.

"Sure." A vague wave of a hand indicated a wide patch of grass beside her.

Megan sat down and looked carefully at the girl. Andrea was right, she was quite pale, and red rims made her eyes look as though she'd been crying. "Suzanne," Megan said, "is something wrong?"

"No." The girl looked straight ahead.

"Are you sure?"

Tears formed and welled in her eyes. "Nothing's wrong," she said firmly. "I'm fine."

An unfamiliar birdsong trilled in the tree above them.

It was pretty, but foreign. Megan wondered if Suzanne was really suffering from homesickness. "You look pretty upset about something," she said. "I won't push, but if you need someone to talk to I'm here, okay?"

"Fine." Suzanne ran her sleeve across her eyes. "Thanks," she added weakly.

Megan eyed her closely. A light wind lifted the girl's dark hair, and blew it back, giving her nothing to hide behind. There were circles like smudges beneath her eyes. She was obviously very upset about something, but she was not a little child. If she wanted to talk, she would. If she didn't, there was no way to force her. Pressing the point would only serve to alienate her.

Megan tried to be light. "It's pretty here, isn't it?"

Another shrug.

Suddenly Megan felt like an intruder. "Suzanne, would you rather be alone right now?"

"I think I'm pregnant." The words were hardly more than a whisper.

"Pregnant?" Megan echoed. The last syllable of the word seemed to disappear into the wind. She looked into Suzanne's eyes and saw how familiar the fear and confusion within them was. Of course. She should have recognized it before. It was something she'd seen in her own mirror for nine months so many years ago. Her heart cried out to the girl. "Suzanne, are you sure?"

Suzanne shrugged and dropped her face into her hands. Her shoulders shook with silent sobs. Megan's breath caught in her throat. She put her arm over Suzanne's trembling back and murmured, "Shhh, shhh, it'll be all right," but she wasn't sure she had the conviction of her words. Knowing what she did of how difficult life was for a young, single woman who found herself with an unexpected pregnancy, how could she say to Suzanne that it would all be all right?

Megan took a deep breath and tried to collect her own emotions. Now wasn't a time for reflection, she told herself, it was time for action. Her own past had no bearing on Suzanne's present or future, and that was all that mattered right now. "Suzanne," she said gently, when the girl's sobs began to subside. Where should she start?

You have listed the father as 'unknown' is that correct?

Megan shuddered as Alma Clancy's voice came back to her from so long ago. She swallowed, trying to keep her focus on what was happening in front of her. Suzanne needed her. It was her chance to help out, perhaps to rectify her own mistakes from the past.

"Suzanne," she said. Her voice was weak. She cleared her throat and tried again, with more force. "I want to help you with this if you'll let me."

Red-rimmed eyes looked at her, filled with such familiar pain. "Really?" She drew in an uneven breath.

"Yes," Megan said firmly. "I really do. Let's talk about it."

"I don't know if I can." The voice was strangled with sobs.

"How about this, if I ask you a question that you're not comfortable with, then you just tell me that you're not ready to talk about it, okay?"

Suzanne nodded.

"Good." She returned to the point that she knew had to come first. "Is the baby's father around? Are you...with him still?"

"He's back home. He...doesn't know."

He doesn't know. What could Megan say to that? Do as I say, not as I did? She didn't have the right to tell Suzanne to tell her boyfriend the truth right away, but she also didn't feel she could sit by and let another teenage girl carry the burden of such a secret for the rest of her life. "Do you plan to tell him?"

"I...I don't know. I guess so. Maybe."

All at once, Megan realized she was in over her head. Granted she had experience with unexpected pregnancy and unwed motherhood, but she didn't know Suzanne very well and she didn't know her boyfriend at all. Their situation may be completely different from Megan's. It probably was.

"I don't want to force him into anything...because of the baby," Suzanne said. "If we're going to be together, I want it to be because he loves me, not because he feels obligated to me."

Off in the distance, a robin soared gracefully over the rolling hills. The motion was carefree in stark contrast to the conversation at hand. "I understand," Megan said. "But there is something to be said for letting people make decisions armed with the facts."

Suzanne sniffed. "You mean you think I should tell him?"

"I can't tell you what to do," Megan said, wishing that after all of her experience she could think of one precious pearl of wisdom which she knew to be true. The only thing that came to her was *tell him so that you don't have to face this music ten years later, when everyone, including your child, might feel betrayed.* "Think carefully about all of this," was all Megan could say. "Think about the future, not just now. And that it's his child too, and he deserves to know the truth." She felt like such a hypocrite.

"But it's my responsibility."

"No, the responsibility belongs to both of you. Unfortunately, though, the burden is on you to break the news and to carry through with whatever you decide."

"He'd be a good dad," Suzanne said with a sniff. "I guess it wouldn't be fair to keep this a secret and not let him have the opportunity to be there for everything."

Megan swallowed. "And to let *yourself* have the opportunity to have the support he can give you. And the support and love he can give the child."

"Yeah, it's not like the baby will be a baby forever. A kid could feel weird not having a dad around when all his friends do."

Megan was glad her students didn't know anything about her personal life, because she wouldn't want

Suzanne to know how close to home she had struck. "That's very true, Suzanne. Very true. If your baby has any chance of having a good relationship with his father, you must allow them both that."

Suzanne frowned. "Sounds like you know someone who's been there."

"Lots of girls have been there, one way or another," Megan allowed. "This is a big deal, certainly, but it's not the end of the world. There are many resources available to you, from medical care to professional counseling to deal with the emotions. You are not alone."

"I know. It just feels like it."

"I know." Megan took her hand and gave it a squeeze. "But you're not."

"I'm sorry to drag you into this."

"You're not, Suzanne. I'm glad you told me about it. I just want to help you think it through now so you don't have a lot of regrets in the future."

Suzanne took a ragged breath. "All I care about is that the baby's healthy and happy. I'll do whatever it takes."

"Good. And I'll help however I can."

"I appreciate that. I'm sure Ted will too. And my parents. Once I break it to them all." Suzanne gave a feeble smile. "Thanks a bunch, Megan."

It was a relief to hear that Suzanne was in a position where she wouldn't have to go through a pregnancy and birth alone. Maybe things would work out for her.

They sat for a few minutes in silence, watching the

birds drift lazily across the sky, then Suzanne said, "I don't want to leave England. Do you think I might be allowed to stay? I mean, with the program, going to classes and all that?"

Megan was about to say of course, when it occurred to her that it might not be that easy. Did London Study have some sort of policy about something like this? It was hard to imagine, but then again, all academic institutions seemed to be extremely careful about their reputations. As modern as the rest of the world was, the collegiate world seemed to lag behind a bit. Was it possible that Suzanne could be expelled from the program in this day and age because she was pregnant?

The thought made Megan cringe.

One man, Megan realized with more than a touch of trepidation, held the answer to that question, and she knew already that she would have to speak with him about this if Suzanne really wanted to stay on. The man who was ultimately in charge of the entire program and everything that went on within it.

Nicholas.

Chapter Nine

Megan went to her room and placed a call to Nicholas's office, but he was gone for the day. She left a message with little hope that she'd hear back from him any time soon, since he was probably gone for the weekend by now. It would have been nice to be able to take some reassurance to Suzanne, but there was nothing more she could do. They'd have to wait. Suzanne would have a lot of waiting ahead of her, Megan thought. Waiting and wondering. She remembered it so well.

After she hung up the receiver, she sat in the glorious room and her thoughts traveled from Suzanne's predicament to her own, so long ago. Suddenly she could think of a hundred ways she could have done things differently.

Yes, she'd written a letter when she found out she

was pregnant. That had been a step in the right direction. But all she had said in her letter was that they had unfinished business and they needed to talk. Nicholas might have thought that meant anything. He might have thought it meant nothing. Certainly he hadn't thought it meant that she was pregnant with his child.

Whatever his reasons for not answering, she had to admit that he probably would have if she'd been more specific.

Afterward, of course, she hadn't felt she could be more specific. How could she possibly tell him she was pregnant when he clearly thought so little of her he wouldn't even answer a letter?

Still, she probably should have made a greater effort to tell him, if not for herself or for him, then at least for William. Her conversation with Suzanne had just reminded her of how her own mistakes had piled up and continued to pile up. The longer she waited, the harder she made it for herself. Even now the weekend stretched endlessly ahead of her. She felt like a thief having William in the house while she kept her secret to herself.

Now that she had decided to tell Nicholas everything on Monday, no matter what interruptions or distractions might come along, she could barely concentrate on her job. Yet she had to do it regardless, she reminded herself, and she had to give it her full attention.

She looked at the mantel clock. She'd already let a couple of hours slip by with her students wandering around by themselves. That might have been okay if they'd known what they were looking at, but so far Megan hadn't given them any instruction at all. She had a list of the various *objets d'art* and antiquities that Nicholas's staff had provided. There were portraits in the great hall and old books in the library.

She thought again of the boy Nicholas had been, and how lonely it must have been to grow up amongst all this austerity. Or, as he might have put it, *tradition*. Had he ever been allowed to run and jump and play as a child, or had he been told to quiet down, to be careful all the time? She couldn't imagine that a child had played in any of the rooms she'd seen so far.

By contrast, when she left her room to get back to work, William was running up and down the halls and slipping on the Oriental carpets.

"Whoa, slow down there kid," she said, noticing a vase wobble on a precarious looking table as he passed. She took him firmly by the shoulders and hoped her voice was softer than her nervous grip. "Don't want to knock anything over here."

"I wasn't gonna," he said breathlessly.

"Not on purpose, maybe, but we can't afford to have an accident." She hated having to stop him from having a good time, especially considering how dull this weekend might be for him. "Now come with me, we're going to look at some pictures."

"Pictures?" he asked skeptically. Obviously it didn't sound like fun. And it probably wouldn't be much fun for him, but she had to keep a close eye on him whether he liked it or not.

"Portraits," she clarified. "And some landscapes, I think. By famous artists. Come with me." They walked through the house, picking up students here and there in the public rooms until she had the whole class collected in the great hall.

Megan led them through it, reading from the list about the paintings and all the great artists who had painted them. It turned out to be quite awe-inspiring, even to William, who had heard of some of the artists himself. One of Nicholas's grandparents had been a real fan of modern work in the early part of the century, and had acquired an entire collection of French surrealist paintings, which added some levity to the tour.

As they entered the library to look at the antique first edition books on the list, one of the girls asked Megan, "Are you going out with the guy who owns this place?"

"No," Megan said, mixed emotions churning to the surface again. "Why?"

The girl looked excited. "Because there's a picture of you with him in *On the Town* this week. They think you might be the next *countess* here. How cool is *that?*"

Megan stood frozen while another student said, "I didn't believe it. I figured you would have said something, if it was true."

"*Is* it true, Mom?" William asked, tugging at her shirt. "Are you really going to be a countess? Are we going to live *here?*"

Until he spoke, she had forgotten he was standing at her side, hearing everything she was.

"No, of course it's not true," she said quickly and tried to laugh. "Not unless I have some birthright I don't know about." She didn't realize what she'd said until the words were out. Her stomach twisted. William might not understand the concept of irony, but she certainly did. All too well.

"Is that possible?" he asked innocently.

"Not for me." She gave him a smile and a pat on the shoulder. "But it's not unheard of."

"Wish it would happen to me," he said. "I want *my* picture in a magazine."

"Maybe someday." She stopped her hands from trembling by holding William's shoulders, and turned to the student who had spoken first. "Do you have a copy of that magazine?"

"There's one right here." She took if off a table and brought it to Megan. "That's what reminded me."

Megan took it in quaking hands.

"It's on page twenty-six."

She turned to the page and saw a picture of herself and Nicholas in the lobby of the theater. It was the one that had been snapped when she looked back out the door at the photographers. It was a very clear image of her face and the headline asked A New Countess At Last?

"That's you, isn't it?"

"It's me. But they've obviously misconstrued what I was doing there." She scanned the brief article.

London—In a rare night on the town, Nicholas Chapman, the Earl of Shrafton, attended the opening of Sir Nigel Drake's *Pygmalion* last Friday night. On his arm was a dishy American, identified only as Megan (pictured above).

The earl declined to comment, but sources close to him suggest that the mysterious Megan is a woman from his past and that the two of them may well be rekindling an old flame. "He prefers Americans," a friend, who asked to remain anonymous, said. "That's one of the reasons he got divorced. There was someone else."

Was this the "someone else"? Only the earl knows, and he's not telling.

It has been nine years since the earl divorced his first wife, Jennifer Sterling-Fox.

Megan set the magazine down. Everyone was looking at her, waiting for a reaction.

"Sounds like they're desperate for a story, even when there isn't one." *And it sounds like Dana Rappaport is desperate to give it to them.* Honestly, she'd barely even changed her wording. How many other people had she told the same thing? *He prefers American girls. Apart from one bad experience, that is.*

"Bummer," someone said. "These are some pretty nice digs."

"Well on Sunday, it's back to our humble abodes." She put her arm around William's shoulder and gave a squeeze, but she couldn't stop thinking about the article. "Sorry, buddy, no fancy title for me."

He mocked a look of profound disappointment. "So we're not moving in here? Those aren't going to be my horses outside?"

There were chuckles from the students, and William smiled, clearly pleased to be entertaining.

"Nope, not today," she said, hoping that if she could sound casual enough no one would give it another thought.

Who was the "someone else" the article—and Dana—referred to? Nicholas had given no indication that his feelings for Megan, or anyone else, had contributed to his divorce.

"Can we get back on topic now?" She walked over to the arched stone fireplace in front of the opposite wall, concentrating on the floor before her, lest her weakened knees collapse and send her sprawling. She located an early edition of Chaucer and called the class over to view it.

While they all perused the ancient pages, she stepped away, ostensibly to examine the objects on the mantel. In reality she was trying to catch her breath and calm her palpitating heart.

As much as she hated to admit it, there was something exhilarating about being photographed with Nicholas and showing up in the glossy pages of a magazine. The article had been kind, and the photo had been reasonably flattering. It was a dream come true for many girls, though Megan couldn't honestly say she'd ever even imagined something like this happening to her.

Which wasn't to say she hadn't imagined making a future with Nicholas. It had been quite a long time since she'd allowed herself to indulge in such fantasies, but she remembered them clearly.

And she was ashamed to admit, even to herself, the number of times over the past couple of weeks that she'd recalled the sight of Nicholas in his tux the night they'd gone to the premiere. Seeing the picture reminded her just how dashing he'd looked and how strong her attraction had threatened to be.

The dream and the reality were having a midair collision.

"Mom?" William interrupted her thoughts before they grew too maudlin. "You're not upset about the magazine, are you?"

"No, why?"

"You look strange. Really pale. I thought maybe you were embarrassed about the picture being in there or something."

She reached out and ruffled his hair. "Not at all, Will, I think it's funny, don't you? Someday it will make an interesting story for us to tell your children."

"My mother, the countess," he said with a laugh.

She winced inwardly. Fortunately she didn't have to respond.

"Oh, *cool*, look at this!" William cried. He knelt in front of the fireplace to examine two intricate gargoyles carved into the stone hearth. "These are really scary looking."

"They're supposed to be." She thanked God that he was young enough to change the subject so readily instead of pursuing the topic of her and Nicholas. "They put them in fireplaces to scare the devil away."

"Think it works?"

"I don't see any devils around, do you?"

No sooner were the words out of her mouth, than Megan got a strange feeling of being watched. She looked up to see Nicholas standing in a doorway not eight feet away, with a leather valise in hand and a very odd look on his face. She could see his chest rise and fall with his breath, but other than that, he was utterly still.

His expression made the hairs on the back of her neck stand up.

Across the vast room the students still oohed and ahhed over the book, apparently unaware of Nicholas's entrance and the pounding of Megan's heart.

"Hello," Megan said at last, but it was more of a question than a greeting.

He didn't answer, and for a moment she wondered if she'd actually spoken aloud.

Then he cocked his head slightly and focused on William, glancing back for a moment at Megan with a silent question in his eyes.

"This is my son, William," she said, in a voice that wasn't quite her own. Did he know? Had he found out somehow? "William, this is Nicholas Chapman. He owns this house."

William looked at him, absently. "Hey," he said,

raising a hand briefly before turning his attention back to the gargoyles.

"Hey," Nicholas repeated softly to him, continuing to study the boy's profile even when William looked away.

Normally Megan would have urged William to be more polite, to thank his host for allowing him to visit, but this time she let it slide. Somehow she felt it would be ridiculous to encourage small talk right now.

"Ms. Stewart?"

A student approached her, completely oblivious to the tension Megan felt had filled the room.

"Excuse me," he said.

Megan tried to compose herself. "Everyone, this is Lord Nicholas Chapman. He owns this estate." The students gave polite responses. Then one said, "Some of us are going to go outside for a walk, is that okay?"

"Fine, yes." She pushed her hair back, an age-old gesture of discomfort that she'd never quite grown out of. "It—it's lovely out there." *Please go,* she implored silently, *all of you, go outside. Let us be alone for this.*

"You know where we'll be if you need us!"

She was vaguely aware of them shuffling out of the room, and the voices of the remaining students talking loudly about the book they were looking at.

Nicholas shifted his gaze from the students across the room back to William.

Megan cleared her throat uncomfortably. He

couldn't know. No one could have told him. The only person who could have said something to him about William was Felicity and Megan was one hundred percent confident that Felicity hadn't revealed a thing to him.

Even as she tried to talk herself out of such paranoia, her nervousness grew. She'd never seen such a look in Nicholas's eyes. As a matter of fact, she'd never seen such a look in *anyone's* eyes. She wasn't even sure how to define it.

When he turned his gaze to her, a tremor rattled through her.

She swallowed. "I didn't expect to see you here," she said. Her voice cracked on the word "you." She was becoming a babbling idiot.

"No." His voice was hard. "I guess not."

It was as if an arc of electricity buzzed between them. It drew her to him even as her instincts told her to turn tail and run.

"Nick, what's wrong?" she asked quietly, moving a couple of feet closer, and wishing they were alone.

He didn't answer, but looked at William again, then fixed his gaze on the wall behind her.

She didn't hear Andrea's approach until she spoke. "Good grief, Ms. Stewart, that painting looks just like your son!"

"What?" She tried to turn her attention away from Nicholas.

"There," Andrea pointed to the spot where Nicholas had been looking. "That portrait. It looks like your son."

By now, the other remaining students had wandered over to see.

"Oh my gosh, it *does*," one of them said.

"It's incredible."

Megan turned as if in slow motion. When she saw what they were looking at, she nearly dropped from shock.

There was a painting over the mantel of a boy standing in front of a pony. It looked to be fairly recent, in the scheme of things, perhaps a century old. The colors were fading but the detail remained precise. She didn't recognize the artist's name, but she certainly recognized the subject.

William.

It wasn't William, of course, but it looked so much like him that anyone looking at them side by side would have believed it was. There was no mistaking the resemblance. From the wavy dark blond hair to the thin, wiry body and the slightly exotic tilt of the eyes, the child was very nearly identical to William.

Megan took a step forward, instinctively trying to block William from Nicholas's view, as if doing so would prevent him from making the connection, but clearly it was already too late.

He knew.

With terrifying deliberation, Nicholas set his valise down and walked toward William. It wasn't more than ten steps but it seemed to take an eternity, as Megan stood frozen to the spot.

When he got to him, he bent down to William's

level. "Are you having a good time here?" he asked William.

Megan began to tremble.

"It's okay," William said. "Not a lot to do here. For kids, I mean."

"No, that's true." Nicholas took a long, slow breath. "How old are you?"

"Ten."

The fact that Nicholas didn't look at Megan was even more nerve-wracking than if he had. Instead he kneeled before his son, looking like the grown-up version of the same person.

"Ten, huh? That's about what I thought." Nicholas nodded, then swallowed.

Megan noticed he tightened his jaw for a moment before ending her ten years of silence with the one simple question that she couldn't prevent William from answering.

"Tell me, son, when's your birthday?"

Chapter Ten

"How could you keep this from me?"

It was thirty-seven minutes later and somehow Megan had gotten her students to go outside and see the old garden maze. She hoped it would hold their attention for at least a little while. Fortunately a couple of the girls who had taken a shine to William offered to take him before Megan even had the chance to ask.

That was one blessing.

"I tried to tell you," Megan said, leaning against the window frame and keeping her gaze fastened on William, who was bouncing around in the distance outside, blissfully unaware of the conversation she and Nicholas—his parents—were having.

"*When?* When did you try to tell me?" Nicholas paced behind the desk. "It's been *ten years!*"

"I wrote you a letter." Megan turned to face him.

Suddenly her shaking subsided and was replaced by an icy calm. "Two months after I got home and found out I was pregnant, I wrote you a letter."

She could tell from the look that crossed his face that he remembered the letter. Clearly.

So much for Felicity's theory that he'd never received it.

He stopped pacing and pointed a finger at her. "That letter didn't say anything about a baby."

Anger boiled in her. "It didn't seem like the kind of thing I should detail in writing for anyone, and possibly everyone, to see."

"No one but me would have seen it."

"Do you know that for sure? I didn't. What if *your fiancée* had seen it?" Megan felt sick, instantly recalling all the mental calculations she'd done when she'd written and sent it. "That kind of thing happens all the time."

"She wouldn't have seen it."

Megan shrugged, exasperated. "I didn't know. For ten years I haven't even known for sure that *you* saw it, because you didn't have the decency to respond." She'd never been one to throw things in anger, but at this moment there was a glass bowl on the desk that looked mighty tempting.

"I couldn't respond." He dropped into the chair behind the desk and looked at her like an insolent child. "What was the point? There was nothing more to say!"

"Yes, Nicholas," she said, her voice low. "There was."

His face colored. "Well, yes, there was as it turns out, but I didn't know that then."

"You would have, if you'd given me just an iota of consideration."

"I would have, if you'd given *me* the slightest indication that you had something more on your mind than what a cad I was for ending our relationship."

"A *cad?*" She placed her hands on the desk and leaned down toward him. "Did you really think I was contacting you at that point to throw some nineteenth century euphemism at you?"

"I didn't know why you were contacting me. That's my point."

She wanted to scream. "Then why didn't you find out? How hard would it have been? How much of your time would it have taken to call me and ask what I needed to discuss with you?" She threw her hands in the air. "Jeez, Nick, didn't you know me well enough to know that I probably had a good reason for asking you to?"

A long moment passed while he looked out the window. "This was important. You should have tried again."

"I was busy with other things, Nicholas. I was nineteen, pregnant and single. I was busy letting my whole family down after they were so proud of me for being the smart, sensible girl who followed the straight and narrow. The first in the family to go to college, although it ended up taking *seven years.*" She shook her head in disgust. "I'm really sorry I didn't take the time and energy to walk through the minefield of your family and marriage to try and coax you into listening to me. It seems I disappointed everyone.''

He gave a single nod. ''All right, you've made your point. It must have been difficult at first. But ten years…''

''Yes, ten years. It took a long time to make life normal again. I had to finish school, to get a job, establish myself in some kind of career so we'd both have some security.''

''I could have helped. I could have seen to it that the child had everything he needed. Everything he wanted.''

She couldn't argue with that. It would be foolish and selfish for her to try and contend that she had done as well by William, financially, as Nicholas could have. ''He had everything he needed,'' she said, not adding that it had sometimes taken a toll on her to ensure that he did.

''Did you? Was anyone there for you?''

She swallowed. ''My parents were there for me. For both of us. We lived with them for the first two years of William's life.''

''As I recall from what you told me, your parents were somewhat old-fashioned. Were they…kind about it?''

She took his meaning immediately and nodded. ''They were as proud of us as they could have been. I never once felt they were ashamed or that they judged me for what happened. It was a very nurturing environment for William. Even once we moved out, they called and came by frequently.''

"I'm glad for that, at least," he said, then paused. "How long were you going to wait before telling me about him?"

She took a short breath, feeling like a fighter in the ninth round. "I'm telling you now. I'm here, aren't I? I brought him here, to England, to you."

"And proceeded to keep him from me."

"We haven't been here that long." She heaved a sigh and slumped down into the chair opposite him. "Look, this isn't the kind of thing I could just announce as soon as I got here. As you know, our conversations haven't been going all that smoothly."

"No," he admitted. "That's true."

"Honestly, I had every intention of telling you everything. Just not this way."

He met her eyes. "Maybe. But that doesn't change the fact that I should have known years ago." His voice had lost some of its contention.

"You can't make me the villain here," she returned. "I did the best I could." She pointed toward the window. "That's a healthy, happy little boy out there. Your son has had a good life so far."

"My son." He looked where she pointed, but she could tell he could no longer see. "I have a son."

Slowly her anger melted into tears, which she tried to blink back. "Yes, your son."

He shook his head to himself. "I've missed so much already."

She hesitated. "I'm sorry you missed his earliest years but he's only ten. It's not too late."

When he turned his gaze to her, Megan realized what was so disconcerting about the way he'd been looking at her in the library. She saw the same thing now. It was complete confusion. Nicholas obviously didn't know what to do. He didn't even know what to feel.

Her heart clenched.

"Look, I have something for you," she said, fighting to keep her voice steady. This wasn't the conversation she'd planned to have, but it was happening anyway so she might as well get it all out. "If you wait here a few minutes, I'll get it."

She hurried to her room and took the photo album out of her briefcase. She hadn't had time to look at it one last time, to put the final touches on, but that was just one more plan that had fallen by the wayside this weekend, and a comparatively small one at that.

When she got back to Nicholas's office, he was exactly as she'd left him, staring out the window, although she noticed that William was no longer in sight. His eyes, while not red, looked stunned.

"This is something I kept for you," she said, handing the book over. "I know it won't make up for the lost time, but..." She shrugged. "It's something, at least. You might find it interesting."

He took the book, as if in a daze, and set it down. "Does he know?" he asked, keeping his eyes on her. "Does he know about me?"

"No." Megan didn't sit down. "I wanted to tell you first."

"Did you imagine that I wouldn't want anything to do with him?"

"I imagined that was a possibility," she admitted. "Yes."

He nodded. "I want as much time with him as possible. How is this going to work?"

From the sound of it, Megan doubted Nicholas had ever in his life had to ask someone else how to do something. "I'm going to tell him about you next," she said.

"Should I be there for that?"

She shook her head. "I think it's best for me to have that talk with him alone."

Nicholas nodded slowly, though she wasn't sure he agreed with her.

"Then what?" he asked.

"Then we take him out together, let him get to know you at his own pace. It may take weeks, or even months, before he's comfortable enough to be alone with you." She didn't add that he might never feel comfortable enough for that at this point. "We'll just have to play it by ear."

"You've thought this through."

"Of course I have. I told you that. It was my intention all along to tell you both the truth."

After a moment, Nicholas asked, "Is this what you wanted to talk about tomorrow?" He smiled then, aware of the foolishness of his question. "Or is there something else?"

She smiled too, glad for the break in tension. "No, this is pretty much it."

Three solid beats passed.

"You realize what this means, don't you?" Nicholas asked seriously. "William is a Chapman, whether by name or not. He's my heir."

"Your *heir*." A tremor ran through Megan. "You mean...legally? All this?" She gestured, indicating the estate.

"That's exactly what I mean."

She put her hand on the chair opposite him and slowly lowered herself into it. She'd hoped he'd accept William as his son, but if he went a step further and named him his heir, the implications were huge. William stood to inherit a considerable estate, not to mention a title. He might eventually move to Britain for good. "Are there no legitimacy issues?" Megan asked. "Isn't this a little too," she searched for the word, "non-traditional for the peerage to accept?"

"I don't give a damn about tradition," Nicholas said in a harsh voice. "Not now. He's my son, damn it. He's going to have everything that goes along with it."

Megan swallowed, well aware of the fact that William's life, and therefore her life with him, was about to change forever. She couldn't stop it. She had no right to stop it. But she was scared. "He's an American, you know. Our home is in America."

"He's half British." Nicholas picked up a pen and nervously tapped it against the desk. "As such, he has several homes here."

Megan felt as if she'd been struck. "What are you saying? If you're implying a custody battle—"

"Of course I'm not," Nicholas said shortly. "I'm not an insensitive lout. I realize I'm a stranger to him."

Relief flooded through her.

"But in eight years he'll be an adult. I'd like for him to have the chance to make an educated choice of where he wants to live and what he wants to do with his life. Don't you?"

"Yes, I do."

"Good. Then we're agreed. Obviously there will be details to work out when your job here ends and it's time for you to return home, but I don't see any reason why we can't work something out so that he can come and visit during holidays."

She tried to imagine what holiday she could stand to endure without William and came up blank. "Perhaps for a week or two in the summer," she offered. "I could stay with Felicity while he visits with you."

Nicholas looked steadily at her. "I have several divorced friends who enjoy their non-custodial times for," he hesitated a fraction of a second, "for dating and what not."

"Are you concerned that your time with William will impede your social life?" she asked, avoiding the topic of her own dating.

"I don't believe I'm going to have enough time with him for that to be even a potential concern," he said dryly. "I meant you."

"Oh. Well, don't worry about my dating life. I'm sure it won't be affected."

"Good," he said curtly.

Was he jealous? It wasn't possible. She dismissed the idea before it could take hold. "I'd better go find William now," she blustered.

He nodded, watching her evenly as she turned to go.

When she was almost to the door, he spoke again.

"What was it like, when you found out that you were pregnant?" he asked.

Megan stopped and turned back. "What?"

Nicholas looked slightly embarrassed. "I shouldn't have asked. I'm sorry."

"No. No, that's okay." She took a few steps back toward him. The subject of her pregnancy was a tender one for her, but never had discussing it seemed more relevant. She forced herself to remember the time, the whole scary, confusing, mystical time. "Apart from the huge anxiety about what was going to happen, it was kind of nice being pregnant with him."

Nicholas smiled briefly then stopped as if he'd decided he shouldn't. He moved away from the desk and took a step closer to Megan. "Did he...did he move around a lot?"

"*Tons*. He was really active."

"Yeah?" He looked pleased. "Active kid, huh?"

"Yes." She smiled, remembering. "I'll never forget, I felt him move for the first time on April 28. My mother had taken me out for lunch at the food court at the mall and at first I just thought it was the gordito I was eating, but then I realized it was the baby." She touched her stomach. "It's like it was just yesterday."

Nicholas looked at her hand, then back into her eyes. "What about when he was born?"

"It was two in the morning, of course." She laughed. It was odd, standing here in the middle of this formal room, telling him these details, but she was touched that he wanted to know them. "My doctor was out of town on, no kidding, a golf trip. So a different doctor came and saw us through the twenty-hour ordeal."

"But there were no complications."

"Not really, no. They had to use suction at the end, and the doctor was actually pushing down on my stomach, but it went pretty quickly from there."

He was silent for a moment, as if trying to imagine the whole thing. "Who was there? I mean, for you."

"My mother was there."

"Good." Some of the pain left his expression. "Who did he resemble most when you first saw him?"

She looked down. "I didn't really see him for the first few hours." Was there any point in telling him about Alma Clancy? Megan decided not. "But when I first saw him I thought he looked like my Uncle Flip."

Nicholas raised his eyebrows. "He looked like an Uncle Flip?"

She laughed at his expression. "Uncle Flip is fat

and bald and at parties when he drinks too much he takes out his teeth."

"Ah. Uncle Flip." Nicholas smiled, looking so deeply into her eyes that she felt like he could see her heart. "My son came out looking like the life of the party. I can live with that."

"He was beautiful," she mused, feeling for the first time the satisfaction of sharing these thoughts with the one person in the world to whom they might mean as much. "Not squished and pointy headed like most babies, but really beautiful, right from day one."

Nicholas's eyes looked a little glassy before he blinked and looked at the floor. "I wish I'd been there."

"There's no point in going there," Megan cautioned. "You know we can't go back. Anyway, everything turned out okay."

His gaze was serious. "I wish I'd been there for you, too, Meg, not just for the baby."

A lump formed in her throat. "*C'est la vie,* eh?"

"It's bad luck," he corrected, with an ironic smile. "Or bad timing."

She thought for a moment. "Maybe. But I wouldn't change it for the world."

He looked chagrined. "No, I didn't mean—"

"I know you didn't." She put a hand on his forearm. "I know. This is hard."

He took her hand in his and put it to his chest, wordlessly.

For the first time in more than ten years, she felt like she was seeing the real Nicholas.

"I suppose we ought to iron out a few logistical details," she said, and instantly regretted it.

Nicholas let go of her hand and went back to his desk, his tone more businesslike. "We should schedule some time for William to get to know me, and vice versa."

"Yes, we'll have to do that." Her hand felt curiously cold.

He leaned back in his chair and studied her from several yards' advantage. "It would be nice if visitation didn't have to mean you or me, as if we were at odds. I always thought that was sad when my friends' children had to go from mother to father and back without any interaction between the two."

She nodded, her heart doing a curious flip-flop. "What else can we do?"

"I don't know, maybe…" He paused. "I don't know. This is all new to me."

"New to me too," Megan said, approaching the desk. She didn't sit down, but stood a couple of feet away looking down at him.

Nicholas frowned thoughtfully. "It is, isn't it? It's just been the two of you for all these years. It must be difficult to contemplate sharing him now."

He'd hit the nail on the head.

"It's not about me," she responded automatically. It was the mantra she repeated every time she began to think about herself instead of William.

"Megan." Nicholas looked her straight in the eye. "Of course it is. It's about you, it's about William,

it's about me too. Everyone's feelings have to matter
here, or no one's going to be happy.''

This was so contrary to what she'd been telling
herself, yet was such a relief, that it took her breath
away. For years she'd berated herself as being selfish
if she indulged even the slightest thought of herself.
''That's nice of you, but—''

''I'm not trying to be *nice*, Megan. It's just common sense.'' Perhaps realizing he was displaying an
uncharacteristic amount of emotion, he added, ''Like
in business.''

She nodded. She hadn't realized how guilty she felt
about keeping William from Nicholas until Nicholas
told her that her feelings mattered. For years she'd
been telling herself that his did not.

''We head back to London tomorrow afternoon,''
she said, unable to contemplate her own feelings right
now. ''I'd like to tell William in private tomorrow
night so that he doesn't have to stifle his feelings,
whatever they are, because of other people being
around.''

''That sounds reasonable,'' Nicholas said.

He didn't add that it would have been nice if he'd
had the same luxury, but Megan thought he must have
felt that way. Certainly she did.

''Then perhaps if you're free Sunday night, we
could take William out to dinner and introduce him
to you properly.'' She smiled, but inside the prospect
of an evening with Nicholas raised a thrill. She tried
to squelch it; this was about William and Nicholas,

not her and Nicholas. "Restaurant food seems to have remarkable powers to smooth things over with him."

Nicholas smiled back. "As I recall, you were not impervious to that particular magic yourself."

Her face grew warm. "He may have inherited your looks, but he has a lot of my temperament." It felt strange to talk to Nicholas this way, as if it was perfectly normal to divvy up her son's genetics. In the years since his birth, she'd barely allowed herself to think about his other heritage.

"I still can't believe all of this," Nicholas said, more to himself than to her.

She didn't know what to say to that.

He turned to her. "I can't wait to get to know him."

A flush of pride and warmth rushed over her. "He's a great kid. But I really better go find him now. He's probably wondering what happened to me."

"Yes, of course." Nicholas picked up his valise. "I'm supposed to get back to London this evening, so I'd better go myself, although it's the last thing in the world I want to do."

She wondered if he had a date, but he answered her question by holding up the valise. "Big meeting," he said. "Eight other people are counting on me to be there. I only came here to pick up some papers I left last weekend. It's lucky I did, though now I hate to leave."

"As far as William's concerned, it's probably for the best," Megan said. "With any luck he won't have given much thought to his resemblance to the picture.

If you go, then no one else is going to notice and comment on his similarity to you. There was a magazine article that speculated on our past and I'd hate for someone to put two and two together before I talk with William.''

He gave a short nod. ''Then I'll go now. But you have my phone numbers. I'd like to hear from you after you've told him. I want to know his reaction.''

''You've got it.'' She smiled, as if all of this was par for the course.

She was almost out the door when Nicholas's voice stopped her again. ''Megan, wait.'' She turned to find him looking pensive.

''Yes?'' she asked, half afraid of what he might have to say.

''The night we went to the premiere,'' he began.

Her shoulders sagged in relief. ''What about it?''

He looked at her. His eyes were curiously clear. ''Nigel asked who the love of your life was.''

She remembered. Her shoulders tensed again.

''You said it was your son's father,'' Nicholas said softly. ''Did you mean it?''

She swallowed, thinking of a thousand responses before settling on the truth. ''Yes. I did.'' She didn't wait for a response. ''Excuse me, now, I really should go.''

She closed the office door behind her and stopped to breathe for a moment. Of all the feelings that danced around within her, the strongest was relief. Relief that the secret she'd kept for so long was out, that she'd finally done the right thing, and that Nicholas wanted to love his son. No sooner did she catch her breath than she heard someone clambering down the stairway and dash across the hall.

"Suzanne?" Megan called, instantly concerned.

Suzanne stopped.

Megan rushed toward her. "Is everything okay?"

Suzanne's face was pink, her eyes bright, but for once it didn't look like she'd been crying. "It's more than okay, everything's *great!*"

This didn't compute. "It is?"

"Yes!" Suzanne laughed. "It was a false alarm. I'm not pregnant."

Megan's knees went weak. "You're not? You're sure?"

"One hundred percent sure." Suzanne giggled again, unable to contain her glee. "In fact, that's why I had to come in for a minute."

Megan understood and gave the girl a big hug. "This is the best news I've heard all week," she said, giving Suzanne an extra squeeze.

When they drew back, Suzanne took Megan's hands in hers. "I don't know how to thank you enough for all of your help."

"I didn't do a thing," Megan said.

"You made me feel like I wasn't alone in the world," Suzanne said. "At a time when I'd never felt so alone in my life. If it weren't for you, I don't know what I would have done."

"You would have done fine, honey," Megan said, a small measure of pride swelling in her chest. "But

I'm so glad you didn't have to make any difficult decisions about your future right now.''

"Me too." Suzanne flashed another smile. "I wish I could repay you somehow."

"You already have. The fact that you trusted me with this was a great compliment."

"You're the best." Suzanne gave her another quick hug. "Are you coming out now? William's trying to talk anyone he can into taking him for a swim." She laughed. "The way he goes on, you'd think he was the Lord of the Manor."

"Someday," Megan murmured, vowing silently that she would never let the obligations he might inherit ruin his life the way they nearly had his father's life.

Chapter Eleven

Although he was surprised, William was nowhere near as shocked as she would have been hearing the same kind of news, or as Nicholas had been. He was, however, somewhat angry with Megan for keeping it from him. That was a reaction she had expected from Nicholas, but not from William.

"Why didn't you tell me this before?" he asked. "All those times I asked you."

"I had to wait until you were ready," she explained. "You're a mature young man now, William, but think about it. Would you have understood this when you were, say, seven?" He always used the age of seven when he was trying to illustrate how much better he'd grown at something.

He thought about it with some seriousness. "No, I guess not."

"I don't think so. Plus, it took me some time to be able to get us here, to England. It would have been hard to learn your father was here and then not be able to get to know him right away." She prodded carefully. "You do want to meet him, don't you?"

"Yes. But he would have come to me," he said, with confidence.

She realized he was probably right. "I'm sure he would have. But it's so much better with us living here for a while."

William frowned. "What happens when we leave?"

It was the one question she didn't have an answer for, though heaven knew she'd given it considerable thought. "We'll have to figure that out as we go along."

Insecurity rose in the boy, she could almost see the baby in him as a familiar worried look came into his eyes. "I don't want to come here without you."

Megan knew that he shouldn't have any fear or feelings of abandonment attached to the introduction of Nicholas. "You won't," she said with conviction. "I will *always* be here for you. You're not losing me, you're just getting someone new in your life. Someone who's going to love you as much as I do, if that's possible."

There was no need to ask herself if Nicholas could be counted on to love his child more reliably than he had loved her. Something inside told her that he would never let William down.

If he did, this time he *would* answer to Megan.

* * *

Nicholas sat in the otherwise-empty sitting room of his London home, looking through the photo album Megan had given him for about the fiftieth time. It was Sunday afternoon, and most of the staff had the day off. He was glad for the privacy, as he had only one hour before going to meet Megan and William at a restaurant near Kensington Palace. He wasn't at all sure how he was supposed to act with William. He knew that Megan would tell him to be himself, but he didn't know who that was anymore.

After years of skimming the surface of life, certain in the knowledge that he was, if nothing else, an honorable man, he was finding out it had all been a lie. He'd made the supreme sacrifice, giving up his own happiness and personal desires for the good of his family, for nothing. When he had resisted contacting Megan after she wrote her letter, he believed he had done the best he could for everyone, including Megan. Contacting her, he believed, would only prolong her pain. And his. It couldn't, he thought, have stopped him from doing what he knew to be the right thing.

He couldn't have been more wrong.

He never dreamed that, in doggedly pursuing the "honorable course of action" he was inadvertently committing the least honorable act of his life. He had left a woman alone and pregnant with his child. He had deprived his child of a father, and of the material comforts he deserved. It was difficult to fully comprehend how much of a struggle it must have been for Megan to have William alone and complete her schooling and begin a career.

He leafed through the album slowly, moved by every image. There was Megan, looking exactly as she had the last time he'd seen her, with a long braid down her back and a rosy complexion, free of makeup. Only she didn't look exactly the same. He didn't know how to guess how pregnant she was, but she had to have been close to the end.

His chest felt tight. He wanted to take that girl, Megan of eleven years ago, and hold her in his arms until all the pain disappeared. He ached for her, and ached for the years they'd missed because of his stupidity. He should have been with her. Until now, seeing these pictures, he hadn't even allowed himself to realize how much he'd missed her when she left.

Life is not a dress rehearsal. Nigel had spewed the cliché at Nicholas more times than he could count, but never had it seemed more true.

He turned back to the book. In another photo, Megan held a tiny baby, swaddled in white blankets. As he flipped the pages, William grew into a white-blonde toddler, standing by a red tricycle under a Christmas tree. His cheeks were flushed red and his eyes were bright little spots. A few more pages, a few more Christmas trees, and William was a few inches taller, blowing out five candles on a birthday cake. The contrast to his own childhood was remarkable.

Megan had given William everything Nicholas could have wished for him to have; love, care, a touch so personal it showed from the birthday cake to the smile on the child's face.

Nicholas's eyes burned. He felt sick. He'd missed so much, all because of his damnable conviction that he was right no matter what. How cocky he'd been about that, even in his misery. He turned the final page and saw a photo of William on his last birthday. He was holding a cake shaped like a car out toward the camera. There was a smudge on one of the wheels, making it obvious that the cake had been homemade. The love that went into it was palpable.

But the most striking thing about the picture was that someone had been cut out of it. Next to William there was the suntanned arm of someone helping hold the cake platter.

Although he could just see her pinkie finger, Nicholas knew that person was Megan.

Why had she gone to the trouble to cut herself out? Even without asking her, he knew the answer.

She didn't think she mattered to Nicholas.

But she did. She mattered more than she could imagine. She mattered more than *he* had imagined. Even with no knowledge of her pregnancy or of William's birth, Nicholas had thought of Megan regularly. Or, rather, he had dismissed the thought of Megan regularly. Every time he wanted to have an interesting conversation; every time their favorite humorist had published a new book, every time the night got late and lonely and he wanted the comfort only a true soul mate could provide.

Ever since she'd arrived back in England, back in

his life, he'd found himself feeling an energy that he hadn't felt in years—eleven years, to be exact. He hadn't put a name to it, hadn't allowed that it was even happening, but he had been happier in the last few weeks just knowing she was near than he had in all the time he'd spent "doing the right thing."

They were history, he told himself. The relationship was long dead. But still, he'd looked forward to seeing her and had gone out of his way on more than one occasion to do so.

And now here was William, a living, vibrant thread between Megan and Nicholas, between then and now. Further proof that the relationship had never died.

But could he convince Megan of that?

He didn't know if he could or not. The only thing he knew with absolute certainty was that he had to try. For the first time in his life he knew what he had to do, and he knew it with both his head and his heart. He had to do his very best to make up for all the lost years, for Megan, for William and also for himself.

"William, you remember Nicholas from the other day, don't you?" Megan said when they met in front of the restaurant. Until this moment, she hadn't considered what William should call him. He couldn't very well start calling him "dad" right off the bat, but "Mr. Chapman" seemed a little too lofty for their relationship, never mind calling him by his title.

So Nicholas it was.

"I remember." William held out his hand. A little man.

Nicholas shook it very seriously. "I'm glad to see you." The smile lines at the corners of his eyes crinkled. The same Nicholas, but older.

Megan's heart constricted.

They went in and sat down at a table near the window. Megan was amazed to see how quickly the two of them hit it off. She barely said a word, but the conversation between Nicholas and William took off. Twenty minutes passed during which they hadn't turned their attention away from each other except to order their food.

"Baseball's a lot better than cricket," William was arguing. "If I come here, I'll have to start my own team because I'm *not* playing cricket."

"You may change your tune once you try it," Nicholas said, but the look on his face said that if he had to hire an entire league of baseball players to make William happy, he'd do it. "What do you say, Megan, think he could be convinced of cricket's merits if he stayed here long enough?"

"We're not staying long enough for that," she joked, but was startled to see what looked like disappointment in Nicholas's eyes.

"How long will you stay?" he asked quietly. "Beyond the end of the semester, or do you plan to leave as soon as it's over?"

It pained her to say, "We're planning to go back when it's over."

Some small, foolish part of her wanted him to object, but instead he just nodded, accepting.

"Then we'll just have to take advantage of the time we have before that."

The waiter appeared and set down heavy white plates of sliced red apple, green grapes, thick crusty bread and wedges of Stilton and cheddar cheeses. There were also several slices of what looked like wilted onion. Nicholas saw William eyeing the latter. "That's pickled onion," he explained, easing nicely into his paternal role.

"Gross!" William said, then flashed a quick apologetic look at Megan for his bad manners. "Does anyone really like to eat it?"

"No one eats it," Nicholas said glibly. "It just gets passed around from plate to plate. Never goes bad, you see, because it's pickled." He took a bite of his cheese and added, "Never gets eaten because it's pickled, too."

William cracked up.

Megan laughed too, pleased with the exchange between the two of them. She had worried that the evening would be thick with awkward silences, especially from William, but it was quite the opposite.

She wished she and Nicholas could have the same easy rapport. More and more over the past several weeks she had grown to miss that and miss him, the *old* him that she caught more and more glimpses of now. Seeing him again reminded her of so many things that had been nice about their relationship. The comfort she'd felt with him. The ability to talk for hours about nothing at all—she'd never experienced anything like that with anyone else. Occasionally she had to force herself to remember how it had ended, but even that memory was fading, being replaced by new memories.

"I don't think I'm going to eat the onion if that's all right," William said.

"I wouldn't either." Nicholas looked at her over William's head and his eyes took on a warmth that she had told herself he no longer possessed. "You've done a great job," he said softly.

"Thanks." She suddenly felt weak and naked under his gaze. She wanted to cuddle William close, for her own security, but she knew it would embarrass him. "I'm sure you will too."

"It's a hard thing to do alone," he answered cryptically.

William interjected something about American football versus English soccer then, and the conversation took off in another direction she didn't care to follow, so Megan sat back and watched the two of them, father and son.

After ten years of worrying about this day and all of the consequences that would come from it, everything had turned out perfectly. William was comfortable, Nicholas was a natural, the future looked like smooth sailing.

So why did Megan feel so empty?

When the phone rang the next night at almost eleven, it nearly scared Megan out of her skin.

"I need to see you." It was Nicholas and from the

sound of the static on the line, he was calling from his car.

"William's staying at a friend's tonight," she said, fighting the thrill that coursed through her at his voice.

"I know, he told me that. I want to see *you*. It's…it's important."

Dread took hold of her. Did he want to talk about custody? About having more custody? "All right." She swallowed hard. "Come on over."

"I'll be there in five minutes."

He arrived faster than that. When he came to the door in faded jeans and an old T-shirt with no jacket on, Megan's internal alarm went off again.

"Nick, what's wrong?"

"Nothing." He ran his hand across his hair. Something it looked like he'd done many times already. "I just need to talk to you."

"About William?"

He shook his head. "About all of us. About you and me."

Her heart tripped. She couldn't help it.

"Let's drive, okay?" He jammed his hands into his front pockets. "There's someplace I'd like to take you, if you don't mind."

The adult in her should have refused, should have said they could sit in the living room and discuss whatever he wanted to discuss rationally. But something else in her thrilled at the idea of going out with him, driving through the inky night alone. Like they used to.

They got in the car and rode for several minutes in silence.

Finally Megan asked, "Where are we going?"

"To the river."

"The river," she repeated. Her voice was thin, like a creaking door that hadn't been opened in years. "Why there?"

"Because that's where *we* are, Megan. We were able to talk there, to be comfortable."

"I'm not sure I'm going to be comfortable there now," she said, so quietly it was almost a whisper. "It's been so long."

"It's been too long," he said, turning the car into the parking lot of the National Theatre, by the Thames.

Five minutes later, they were walking along the bank of the river toward Waterloo Bridge, feet crunching in the pebbly sand beneath. The sky was clearing after four days of rain, and tiny stars winked between patches of cloud.

Megan ached with mixed feelings of anticipation and fear. "This is familiar," she understated.

He laughed softly. "I haven't done this in years."

"Isn't this where you bring all your girls?" she asked, half kidding.

"Megan." He knocked his arm lightly against her shoulder and continued to look straight ahead. "If I didn't know better, I'd say you were jealous."

The warmth of his body penetrated her sleeve, drawing her to him. For a second she could almost believe it was eleven years ago and they were both still young, still unencumbered by pain, still in love. The warmth beneath his touch spread through her body, though she tried to resist it. "I'm not jealous. You can do whatever you want."

"Even if it includes you?"

She glanced at him, then back at the skyline, hoping he would keep his hand on her. Even that small touch made her feel steady in a moment that threatened to rock her whole world. She didn't know what he was intimating, or if he was intimating anything at all. She was afraid to ask, for fear of a disappointment she might never get over. "This whole scene feels like a book I set down halfway through," she said quietly.

He stopped and looked at her. Behind him, the lights of the city sparkled off the water. "Are you willing to pick it up and keep reading?"

Her heart sang, then hit a note of apprehension. "Is that what you wanted to talk to me about?"

"Yes."

Megan took a deep breath of the damp, balmy air. "You don't have to do this. You can spend whatever time you want with William, you know."

"*This* isn't about William," Nicholas objected. "William's damn important, but this is about you and me. I'm tired of us misinterpreting each other's feelings. How do you really feel about *me?*"

"I'm afraid." Inside, she was aware of a small, unrealistic wish for him to do something—anything— to make it all right again.

They took a few more steps, then he said, "I am too."

"You? I didn't think anything scared you."

"Only you scare me."

"Why?"

"Because my feelings for you are the one thing I cannot control." He stopped and turned to face her. "I never could, though God knows I tried."

Heart pounding, she looked across the murky water to the ghostly gothic houses of Parliament. She didn't trust herself to look at him. "It took a long time to get over you. I don't want to go through it again."

"There's very little I can say to reassure you," he said. "Except that I didn't know, then, that it would matter so much. Every decision I made was the wrong one and I know it now." He held her by the shoulders, a little too tightly.

She was exhilarated and afraid. How could she give in to him after all this time?

How could she not?

She'd dreamed of this moment for years and now it felt too good to let it go.

"You said you cared about me before, Nicholas. It didn't seem to matter in the end."

In the distance, there was a hum of cars speeding across the bridge. "I was young, or youngish." He laughed without a trace of humor, then tossed a stone and watched intently as the ripples fanned out toward the shore. "And I was foolish."

Megan bent to pick up a stone. "You won't get an

argument from me on that." She tossed it. The stone plopped in the river and sank to the bottom.

"I'm not so young anymore," he said, putting his hand on her shoulder and turning her to face him. "And I'm not quite as foolish. The only thing that remains the same is that I love you. I've loved you for years, Megan, and fought it every step of the way."

Megan's resolve to resist him evaporated. She swallowed, hard, then swallowed again. No words would come to her.

"I know that's probably not what you wanted to hear," Nicholas said. "But I had to tell you. To find out if there's even a chance that we might still have a future together. To find out if you could ever forgive me and let me try to make it up to you."

She studied the reflection of the buildings in the water, afraid to look at him for fear this would all turn out to be a mistake. "You're sure this isn't because of William?"

"Absolutely. Finding out about William is the best thing that ever happened in my life, but as far as our relationship goes, it only served to open my eyes to something I should have seen all along." He took her arm and held it, looking deeply into her eyes. "That you are the only woman I will ever love and I need you in my life and that's worth a hell of a lot more than tradition, business, or so-called family honor. I've lived a lie for ten years. I want to live the truth now, and the only way I can do that is with you."

A knot of emotion forced its way into Megan's throat.

"I...I..." She didn't know what to say. Suddenly, she didn't even know what to feel.

At that moment, Big Ben rang its familiar dirge, followed by several steady gongs.

"I can't help but feel my carriage is about to turn to a pumpkin," Megan laughed nervously.

"Sometimes it works the other way around," Nicholas said. "Look, over there." He pointed. "Remember that?"

Megan looked at the familiar silhouette of St. Paul's. "It hasn't changed. It probably never will." She gave an ironic laugh. "There's probably one thing in the world I can depend on, and it's St. Paul's."

"You can depend on me."

"Can I?"

He looked at her, then back at St. Paul's. "I think of you," he said, "every time I see that." He gave a mirthless chuckle and shook his head. "I grew up in this bloody city, with that bloody skyline, my whole life, yet for the past ten years when I look at it all I see is you." He looked at her. "Yes, you can depend on me."

All the love she'd been denying came surging forth in her. "I want to." There was a catch in her voice.

"Then do."

His gaze intensified, like a fire catching on dry paper. He leaned close, his mouth almost touching hers, and said, "Stay with me."

A long shiver ran through her as his warm breath tickled against her face. She opened her mouth to respond, but he covered it with his own.

A shudder of pleasure shook her and she felt his arms close around her, drawing her closer. His lips were warm and tender and they moved against hers in a motion so familiar it made her want to cry. How long had she dreamed of this moment? How many times had she chastised herself, believing it would never happen?

Was it really happening now?

Dizzying currents of desire buzzed through her. Her knees felt weak. If it weren't for his arms, holding her so tightly, she might have collapsed.

He drew a finger along her spine, leaving a tingling trail where his touch passed. All her arguments against loving him evaporated. She did love him. She'd always loved him. She always would.

He ran small kisses along her jawline and down to her neck. He touched a sensitive spot between her neck and shoulder and she sighed, giving in to him fully.

This, she realized on a deep level, was what she'd been waiting for for years. Somewhere in the back of her mind, despite her frayed emotions, she had thought of Nicholas's kiss over and over again, longing for it as one would long for water in the desert.

And it was every bit as satisfying.

She ran her hands slowly up his smooth, muscular back and buried her fingers in his hair. It was exactly as she remembered...or was it that she'd imagined?

After all the thoughts of him that she'd dismissed over the years, it was hard to say what was memory and what was fantasy.

Now it all felt like fantasy. Like a glorious dream, in vivid color. Every sense was overflowing. If they stayed a hundred years, she felt she still couldn't get enough of him.

The way he kissed her, it seemed as if he felt the same. There was an urgency to it she'd never experienced before. They held each other tightly, clasped together almost in desperation.

How long they stood there, she couldn't say.

Finally he drew back, leaving Megan breathless and weak. It took her a moment to regain her composure before he stunned her again.

"Marry me."

"What?" she gasped.

"Marry me," he repeated, then dropped to his knees before her. "Please marry me. Perhaps I have no right to ask, but I promise you I'll spend the rest of my life trying to make you happy. You will never have cause to doubt me again."

Somehow she believed him. And it wasn't just because she wanted to.

"Please," he repeated. "Grow old with me. Say you'll marry me."

She smiled through tears that flowed freely down her cheeks. "I will."

He stood up and took her in his arms again, kissing her until an older couple walked by and made a derogatory remark about public displays of affection.

Stifling her laughter, Megan drew back and gave a little wave as the woman turned to give them one more disapproving glance.

"Get used to it," Nicholas said, but only so Megan could hear. "It's going to be happening a lot from now on." Megan laughed and asked, "What about William?"

"He'll have to get used to it too." Nicholas smiled.

"I mean, should we call him? Have him come home and tell him the news?"

"We'll tell him the news in the morning," Nicholas said, taking her hand in his, and leading her back toward the car. "Tonight will be just for us."

Epilogue

"Okay, Megan, I give up. Why are you bringing me here?"

"I told you, I have a surprise for you." Megan laughed and squeezed Nicholas's hand as she led him across Waterloo Bridge on foot.

A car whizzed by. "I'll be surprised if we don't get killed." Nicholas laughed and caught Megan around the waist, whirling her around to face him. "But to die with my one true love..."

"Stop it." She swatted at him playfully. "We're not going to get run over." She kissed him quickly on the lips.

He caught her as she tried to pull away and deepened the kiss. For minutes they stood there, oblivious to the cars and everything else, until finally Megan pulled back.

"Just a few more feet," she said, pulling him forward. She stopped when the dome of St. Paul's was centered perfectly before them. This was where she wanted to do it. "How many times do you think we stood here together?" she asked, looking across the water. "I never dreamed we'd be married in St. Paul's one day."

"I didn't either, but we've got the pictures to prove it." He put his arm around her and she shrugged into the comfortable niche.

She sighed, for a moment willing to stay like this forever. But then she remembered that Nigel and William were going to come out of the National Theater to meet them any minute and she wanted to tell Nicholas her news in private.

He kissed her head. "So what's this all about?"

She took a step away and looked up at him. "Well, I have some news and I wanted to do this right this time."

His eyes widened.

She took his hands in hers.

"Are you saying…?" He didn't finish, but the gleam in his eyes made it clear that he hoped she was.

She nodded. "We're going to have another baby."

Nicholas let out a whoop that rivaled Big Ben's chime. "Another baby! Are you sure?"

"Absolutely."

He pulled her into his arms and held her tightly. "I'm going to be there for you every second this time. I'm going to every doctor's appointment, every test, everything. You'll be so sick of me by the time this baby comes you'll want to move to the country house.''

She laughed and held on to him. "I doubt that."

"Mom! Dad!"

They broke away and saw William running toward them across the bridge. Nigel walked with slow dignity behind him, tipping his hat when they turned.

"What's going on?" William wanted to know. "What's the big surprise?"

"Yes, indeed, what is this surprise?" Nigel asked, with an expression that said he knew exactly what it was. "I've heard of little else all evening. This boy is even more single-minded than his father."

"The surprise is—"

"You're going to have a baby!" William finished, then burst into gales of laughter.

"How did you know that?" Nicholas asked him, ruffling his hair. He looked at Nigel, who merely shrugged.

"I was with Mom when she bought the test." He smiled at Megan. "You're not very good at being secretive, Mom."

"She fooled me," Nicholas said, beaming.

"Well, this calls for a celebration," Nigel said broadly. "Champagne and ginger ale all around, what do you say?"

"Yes!" William cried. "And cake?"

"Mmm, cake sounds really good," Megan said.

"You've got it." Nicholas took her hand and William's and said to Nigel, "Let's take my wife and children to the Ritz and stuff them with delicious food, what do you say?''

''I could do with a bite myself,'' Nigel said, hooking his arm through Megan's. ''But this exercise is killing me. I do hope your car is parked at the end of the bridge.''

Nicholas laughed and nodded, and the four of them set out walking to the bank of the river and to their future.

*   *   *   *   *

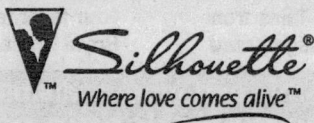

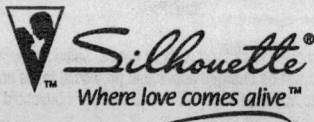

If you enjoyed what you just read,
then we've got an offer you can't resist!

Take 2 bestselling
love stories FREE!
Plus get a FREE surprise gift!

Clip this page and mail it to Silhouette Reader Service™

IN U.S.A.	IN CANADA
3010 Walden Ave.	P.O. Box 609
P.O. Box 1867	Fort Erie, Ontario
Buffalo, N.Y. 14240-1867	L2A 5X3

YES! Please send me 2 free Silhouette Romance® novels and my free surprise gift. After receiving them, if I don't wish to receive anymore, I can return the shipping statement marked cancel. If I don't cancel, I will receive 6 brand-new novels every month, before they're available in stores! In the U.S.A., bill me at the bargain price of $3.15 plus 25¢ shipping and handling per book and applicable sales tax, if any*. In Canada, bill me at the bargain price of $3.50 plus 25¢ shipping and handling per book and applicable taxes**. That's the complete price and a savings of at least 10% off the cover prices—what a great deal! I understand that accepting the 2 free books and gift places me under no obligation ever to buy any books. I can always return a shipment and cancel at any time. Even if I never buy another book from Silhouette, the 2 free books and gift are mine to keep forever.

215 SEN DFNQ
315 SEN DFNR

Name	(PLEASE PRINT)	
Address		Apt.#
City	State/Prov.	Zip/Postal Code

* Terms and prices subject to change without notice. Sales tax applicable in N.Y.

** Canadian residents will be charged applicable provincial taxes and GST.

All orders subject to approval. Offer limited to one per household and not valid to current Silhouette Romance® subscribers.

® are registered trademarks of Harlequin Enterprises Limited.

SROM01 ©1998 Harlequin Enterprises Limited

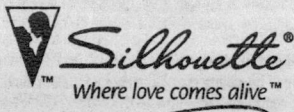

HARLEQUIN "SILHOUETTE MAKES YOU A STAR!" CONTEST 1308
OFFICIAL RULES
NO PURCHASE NECESSARY TO ENTER

1. To enter, follow directions published in the offer to which you are responding. Contest begins June 1, 2001, and ends on September 28, 2001. Entries must be postmarked by September 28, 2001, and received by October 5, 2001. Enter by hand-printing (or typing) on an 8 ¹/₂" x 11" piece of paper your name, address (including zip code), contest number/name and attaching a script containing 500 words or less, along with drawings, photographs or magazine cutouts, or combinations thereof (i.e., collage) on no larger than 9" x 12" piece of paper, describing how the Silhouette books make romance come alive for you. Mail via first-class mail to: Harlequin "Silhouette Makes You a Star!" Contest 1308, (in the U.S.) P.O. Box 9069, Buffalo, NY 14269-9069, (in Canada) P.O. Box 637, Fort Erie, Ontario, Canada L2A 5X3. Limit one entry per person, household or organization.

2. Contests will be judged by a panel of members of the Harlequin editorial, marketing and public relations staff. Fifty percent of criteria will be judged against script and fifty percent will be judged against drawing, photographs and/or magazine cutouts. Judging criteria will be based on the following:

   - Sincerity—25%
   - Originality and Creativity—50%
   - Emotionally Compelling—25%

   In the event of a tie, duplicate prizes will be awarded. Decisions of the judges are final.

3. All entries become the property of Torstar Corp. and may be used for future promotional purposes. Entries will not be returned. No responsibility is assumed for lost, late, illegible, incomplete, inaccurate, nondelivered or misdirected mail.

4. Contest open only to residents of the U.S. (except Puerto Rico) and Canada who are 18 years of age or older, and is void wherever prohibited by law; all applicable laws and regulations apply. Any litigation within the Province of Quebec respecting the conduct or organization of a publicity contest may be submitted to the Régie des alcools, des courses et des jeux for a ruling. Any litigation respecting the awarding of a prize may be submitted to the Régie des alcools, des courses et des jeux only for the purpose of helping the parties reach a settlement. Employees and immediate family members of Torstar Corp. and D. L. Blair, Inc., their affiliates, subsidiaries and all other agencies, entities and persons connected with the use, marketing or conduct of this contest are not eligible to enter. Taxes on prizes are the sole responsibility of the winner. Acceptance of any prize offered constitutes permission to use winner's name, photograph or other likeness for the purposes of advertising, trade and promotion on behalf of Torstar Corp., its affiliates and subsidiaries without further compensation to the winner, unless prohibited by law.

5. Winner will be determined no later than November 30, 2001, and will be notified by mail. Winner will be required to sign and return an Affidavit of Eligibility/Release of Liability/Publicity Release form within 15 days after winner notification. Noncompliance within that time period may result in disqualification and an alternative winner may be selected. All travelers must execute a Release of Liability prior to ticketing and must possess required travel documents (e.g., passport, photo ID) where applicable. Trip must be booked by December 31, 2001, and completed within one year of notification. No substitution of prize permitted by winner. Torstar Corp. and D. L. Blair, Inc., their parents, affiliates and subsidiaries are not responsible for errors in printing of contest, entries and/or game pieces. In the event of printing or other errors that may result in unintended prize values or duplication of prizes, all affected game pieces or entries shall be null and void. **Purchase or acceptance of a product offer does not improve your chances of winning.**

6. Prizes: (1) Grand Prize—A 2-night/3-day trip for two (2) to New York City, including round-trip coach air transportation nearest winner's home and hotel accommodations (double occupancy) at The Plaza Hotel, a glamorous afternoon makeover at a trendy New York spa, $1,000 in U.S. spending money and an opportunity to have a professional photo taken and appear in a Silhouette advertisement (approximate retail value: $7,000). (10) Ten Runner-Up Prizes of gift packages (retail value $50 ea.). Prizes consist of only those items listed as part of the prize. Limit one prize per person. Prize is valued in U.S. currency.

7. For the name of the winner (available after December 31, 2001) send a self-addressed, stamped envelope to: Harlequin "Silhouette Makes You a Star!" Contest 1197 Winners, P.O. Box 4200 Blair, NE 68009-4200 or you may access the www.eHarlequin.com Web site through February 28, 2002.

Contest sponsored by Torstar Corp., P.O Box 9042, Buffalo, NY 14269-9042.

SRMYAS2

Babies are en route in a trio of brand-new stories of love found on the way to the delivery date!

Labor of Love

Featuring

USA Today bestselling author
Sharon Sala

Award-winning author
Marie Ferrarella

And reader favorite
Leanne Banks

On sale this July at your favorite retail outlet!

Only from
Silhouette Books

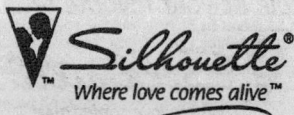

Where love comes alive™

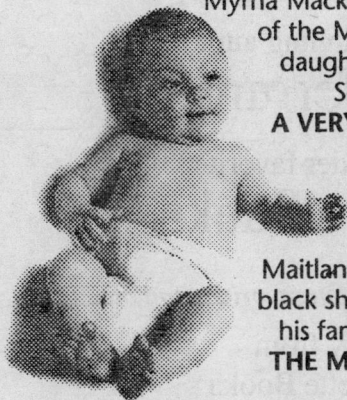

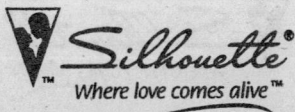